BATTLETECH:
MARAUDER
A BATTLETECH ANTHOLOGY

BY LANCE SCARINCI

BATTLETECH: MARAUDER
By Lance Scarinci
Cover art by Florian Mellies
Interior art by Joel Biske, Alan Blackwell, Chris Daranouvong, Brent Evans, Harri Kallio, Duane Loose, Chris Lowrey, Jim Nelson, Matt Plog, Anthony Scroggins, Franz Vohwinkel
Cover design by David Kerber

©2022 The Topps Company, Inc. All Rights Reserved. *BattleTech & MechWarrior* are registered trademarks and/or trademarks of The Topps Company, Inc., in the United States and/or other countries. Catalyst Game Labs and the Catalyst Game Labs logo are trademarks of InMediaRes Productions LLC. No part of this work may be reproduced, stored in a retrieval system, or transmitted in any form or by any means, without the prior permission in writing of the Copyright Owner, nor be otherwise circulated in any form other than that in which it is published.

Printed in USA.

Published by Catalyst Game Labs,
an imprint of InMediaRes Productions, LLC
5003 Main St. #110 • Tacoma, WA 98407

CONTENTS

FOREWORD

I've read quite a few of Lance Scarinci's stories over the years, and I've even had the privilege of publishing a handful of them myself, in anthologies and in issues of *Shrapnel*, the Official *BattleTech* Magazine. Lance writes memorable, engaging characters, and I always get excited when one of his tales hits my desk. But the stories of his that always stuck with me the most throughout the years were the ones about a rather unusual character: an all-black *Marauder*, a strange BattleMech that seemed to defy all attempts at understanding where it came from and what makes it work.

Even during my early days with BattleCorps, we tried to steer people away from sending story submissions that firmly fell outside the general aesthetic of *BattleTech*, such as stories of a different genre, where any *BattleTech* content was an afterthought. At the end of the day, the *BattleTech* universe is military sci-fi mixed with Machiavellian politics: it revolves around giant, stompy war machines and chronicles futuristic combat and the people who direct those conflicts. But can good *BattleTech* stories include *elements* of other fiction genres, like horror or romance? Absolutely. The pieces contained in this volume are a great example of this sort of idea: military sci-fi as seen through the lens of the horror genre. And it works. The ghost stories in this collection will certainly send a bit of a chill down your spine, and make you wonder just what truly drives the titular 'Mech.

The first story in this anthology—"Marauder," first published on BattleCorps in 2010—certainly set a precedent for genre blending in *BattleTech* fiction, and its influence is still felt to this day, even among other *BattleTech* authors. (For example,

Michael J. Ciaravella's "Devil Take the Hindmost," a story about an unsettling *Atlas* on Solaris VII, appeared in *Shrapnel* #2, and was specifically written to be a spiritual successor to the stories contained in this collection.) This collection also includes "Kindred Soul" and "Ravager," both of which were also published on BattleCorps, in 2012 and 2014, respectively. The final story, "Ghost Hunting," is a brand-new piece written specifically for this collection, and it shows the so-called Black *Marauder* having become a thing of legend, one spoken about in hushed whispers in fear of drawing its attention.

For those looking for future stories about the Black *Marauder*, look no further than *Shrapnel*, which will feature the brand-new story "Wolf Pelts and Raven Feathers" in issue #10, available Fall 2022. And beyond that, if you have the courage to write your own tale about the Black *Marauder*, I dare you contribute to the growing legend by submitting your story to Shrapnel here:

https://pulsepublishingsubmissions.moksha.io/ publication/shrapnel-the-battletech-magazine-fiction/ guidelines

Philip A. Lee
Managing Editor of *Shrapnel*, the Official *BattleTech* Magazine

INTRODUCTION

LANCE SCARINCI

For as long as I can remember, I wanted to tell stories. Problem was, for the first three and a half decades of my life, I wasn't very good at it. I had a lot of decent ideas, but getting them out was like passing a DropShip-sized kidney stone.

Around late 2009, I decided if I was ever going to make a go at it I'd better get started, or just give it up entirely. Luckily, BattleCorps accepted new writers for *BattleTech* fiction, so I dusted off an old journal containing a fragment of a story I'd scribbled down, and dared myself to finish it. In a few weeks, I had something workable. There was no magic, no sudden genius, just a lot of hard work, study, and revision. At the end of it, I had something passable, and Jason Schmetzer, the managing editor of BattleCorps, thought so too, because he bought it. That story was simply titled "Marauder." It is the first story I ever wrote, the first I ever sold, and I'm proud to see it here, launching this collection.

I've loved the *BattleTech* universe since I discovered it in 1989. One of my favorite aspects has always been the great mysteries hidden in the fiction. The Vandenburg White Wings, the Disappearing Battleship of Merope, the Minnesota Tribe. One by one, many of these mysteries were solved. With the Black *Marauder* series, I wanted to help refill that vessel while also delving into a part of *BattleTech* left largely unexplored: MechWarrior superstition. I wanted to give the sense that there are things out there in the deep, endless black that humankind is not prepared to meet, even with an army of BattleMechs. So I gave people a haunted 'Mech.

I wrote three stories chronicling the 'Mech I named the Dark One, but the fanbase has taken to calling the Black *Marauder*. Each story focuses on a different aspect of one overall tale. "Marauder" is the story of the 'Mech; "Kindred Soul" is the story of the man, Kevin Langstrom; "Ravager" presents the perspective of those standing in the Dark One's shadow. I've been humbled by the fan reaction these stories. I've seen artwork and amazing miniatures based on them, and every year I still get several inquiries on where to find these tales. They've been unavailable since BattleCorps went offline, but now I finally have a place to point the curious. As an added bonus, presented here for the first time is a fourth perspective on the Dark One: "Ghost Hunting" tells the tale of those who would dare hunt this unholy beast.

I hope you find something inspiring in my stories, be it a nemesis for your tabletop games, ideas for your role-playing game, or just a desire to know more about the *BattleTech* universe. Maybe you'll finally sit down and pound out your own story. That would make me happy. And if you get to the end and find yourself wanting more tales of the Dark One, well...you won't be disappointed. I'd like to thank Jason Schmetzer for giving me my break so long ago, John Helfers for agreeing to publish this collection, and Phil Lee for being a good friend and editor. And Johannes Heidler, for all these years of encouragement.

Now my fellow *BattleTech*ers, read and enjoy! And remember, *BattleTech* is a sci-fi setting grounded in reality, but what actually is real?

MARAUDER

PADISHAN FLATS
WARREN
CAPELLAN MARCH
FEDERATED SUNS
8 DECEMBER 3073

"Here we are," Grange said as they rounded a final bend.

Kevin didn't think "here" looked particularly inviting. Set against a large hill, the ferrocrete building looked more stable than anything in the wrecked town they'd just passed through, but not much. Its pockmarked walls blended smoothly into the natural rock, time and dust coloring them the same red as the surrounding desert. A pile of twigs that might have been a bird's nest poked from the eaves, and boards covered the windows and single door, bleached by the sun until they resembled old bones. Some had split or fallen off, revealing the shadowy depths within.

"Sorry, Sarge, I didn't hear you properly," Kevin said. "I thought you said we were going to get a 'Mech, not a wreck."

That's what the trek was supposedly about. One BattleMech. A full battalion of them waited back at the garrison, most in good working order. Kevin didn't think heading off into the godforsaken desert to get just one more was worth the trouble, yet here he was, bouncing along the remains of this road in a dirty old jeep, with a load of high explosives in the back. That made him nervous, especially considering the quality of Grange's driving.

He hadn't questioned the old sergeant when they'd loaded the cases up under the quartermaster's watchful eye just before sunrise. Grange wasn't the kind of man who invited questions. You either did what he told you to, or you did what he told you to with some bruises and an extra punishment assignment. Even as old as he was, Grange packed a mean right hook. Barracks rumor said he had perfected it during the Reunification War.

"Shut your trap, son," the old sergeant growled. It was the longest sentence he'd spoken since they had left the base.

Although his long-winded war stories were the stuff of legend, today the old man had uncharacteristically hidden his rugged face behind a wrap-around visor and answered any inquiries with a disinterested grunt. After a while, Kevin gave up and entertained himself by counting the potholes Grange hit, giving double points for the ones the old man could have avoided if he'd bothered to turn the wheel. It was not an insignificant number.

They bumped over a set of tracks that led into a deadfall, and pulled up to the building. When Grange shut the jeep down, its engine pinged a couple of times, and the radiator hissed in relief. The early morning heat was just beginning to get uncomfortable. It sucked Kevin's energy away, and he had been fighting hard not to nod off for the past few miles.

Grange leaned on the steering wheel, sucking in a huge breath and expelling it through puffed cheeks. He looked the way Kevin usually felt after one of the sergeant's own workouts. Maybe the heat was getting to him, too.

"So, what's this place?" Kevin asked.

"A graveyard," Grange said.

"A what?"

"Not in the literal sense," Grange said with a wry smile. He climbed out and walked to the back of the jeep, where he removed a pry bar from the kit box. "More in the sense it's a place you put something you want to forget. Something you want to bury, and hope it stays buried."

"Sounds promising," Kevin said. To him, the whole world of Warren was a place where things went to be buried and forgotten—like his career. But that's what happened when you graduated in the bottom third of a class from a second-rate academy. You don't get to go to the Brigade of Guards or the Avalon Hussars, you get to go to the Capellan March Militia and guard the Warren Polymorphous Defense Zone, in the backwater of the Federated Suns.

Kevin hated this world, hated being stuck here. War with the Capellans, the Blakists, and now the Taurians had distracted the powers that be, and all his applications for transfer, all the recommendations from superior officers had been swept under the rug. New recruits from respected universities replenished the ranks, while the militia stayed put. Only an act of God was going to get him recognized, give him a chance to get off this rock and into a real unit.

The people he vented his frustrations to were no help either. Most told him this assignment was his own fault. He could have studied harder, not spent so much time goofing off, or wrapped around the girl of the moment. He could have applied to a real academy like Warrior's Hall, or maybe even Albion. None of that had seemed so important back then, but five years as MechWarrior Corporal Langstrom, Second Battalion, Third Company, Warren Capellan March Militia, reporting to Sergeant-Major Grange, had changed his mind.

Kevin was savvy enough to hide his resentment from the people he served with. He was smarter than this outfit full of inbred Outbackers and retirees, better than them. Few of them knew it, but Grange did. He treated Kevin differently than the rest of his charges, showed him a little more respect. Maybe the old man recognized his wasted potential and tried to make up for it in his own small way, or maybe Kevin really did remind him of his long dead son, as one old hand had suggested.

Grange took a few more items from the kit box, including a pair of tiny flashlights and a smaller pry bar, which he gave to Kevin. "Gotta lot of work ahead. Let's get started before this damned sun gets too hot."

"Well, I hope you packed lunch." Kevin hefted his pry bar, walking alongside Grange to the boarded door.

"Rations," Grange replied, digging his bar into the old wood.

Of course. The old man lived on the damn things. They were probably the only thing he'd eaten for the past fifty years.

The last board slid off its nails with a dry squeak. Grange tossed it aside and studied the battered door. The outline of an old, faded logo was barely visible, its colors bleached away by the desert sun long ago. Dulled graffiti and even a few bullet holes added to its character.

"This used to be a gold mine back in the Star League days," the old sergeant said. "Then the vein played out some time in the twenty-ninth century, and the company shut 'er down and abandoned the place. A lot of people were put out of work. The town faded away not much later. People pretty much forgot about it, except for the occasional kids looking for a hangout. A local gang staked it out as their personal turf about forty years ago. Ran their own miniature crime wave out of here, until the law had enough and burned them out.

"I used to come here when I was a kid, hoping to find traces of gold for myself, but there was nothing to be had. Nothing but dust and memories." He smacked his hands together, removing the dust. "Nobody comes here now. Few people even remember it exists, and that suits me just fine."

Sand had frozen the lock, so they broke down the door with a makeshift battering ram. It collapsed off its ancient hinges after just two heaves. They entered a dingy antechamber that may once have been a reception area. Grange lit his small flashlight and led the way through a complex that extended into the mountain. Graffiti covered almost every surface, broken occasionally by scorch marks and the odd bullet hole. Debris, some of it identifiable as office equipment, crunched underfoot. Several walls had collapsed, and the ceiling buckled alarmingly in some places. Still, the place had a sense of dignified history. Fortunes had been won here.

Grange led Kevin to a room set far back from the entrance where the sun didn't reach. Stale air pressed in, and his tiny flashlight felt woefully inadequate. On one wall stood a door more modern than the rest of the complex: solid looking, like a vault door, with large hinges and a long metal handle. A security keypad glowed red on the wall beside it.

Grange grunted in satisfaction. "Generator's still running."

The keypad looked very out of place amid this seemingly worthless devastation. It piqued Kevin's curiosity. "That's some heavy security, Sarge. I thought you said no one came here anymore."

"Nobody I know about. Doesn't mean I know everything. Last thing I want is someone just stumbling in here." Grange blew on the numbers. Dust swirled, and Kevin covered his nose.

"You remember the combination?" he asked, only half jokingly.

The old man grunted again. "Some things you don't forget, even if you try." He pressed a few buttons. The sequence meant nothing to Kevin, but the pad beeped, changing from red to green. A dull *clunk* sounded from within the wall.

Grange turned the long handle and dragged the door open to reveal a deep, black cave. It grated loudly as it moved, the noise echoing back from inside. Cool, dry air fluttered around them. As it worked into Kevin's lungs, he found he didn't really want to explore the depths it came from.

Grange groped along the wall until he found a power switch. When he flipped it, a series of dim sodium lights flared, pushing back the endless dark. They were in a cavern, a vast, man-made edifice hewn from the heart rock of the mountain. The decrepit series of rails they'd crossed outside continued here, emerging from under the deadfall and disappearing into the depths. This was unmistakably the old mine's main entrance.

Signs of ancient habitation were present in the form of fire-blackened barrels ringed by crates and large rocks, the remains of makeshift campsites. Old food and beverage containers littered the floor, and a pyramid-shaped can of Pharaoh beer sat on the end of a rail cart as if someone had just placed it there. The air was still and oppressive, the cave very empty.

Almost empty. Off to one side, something lurked in the shadows where the pools of light didn't seem to reach. It drew Kevin's attention with a sudden spike of adrenaline. He squinted, but couldn't quite make out what it was, save that it was huge. It remained little more than a shadow, black against the charcoal of the walls.

Grange strode straight toward the object, stepping carefully through the detritus. Kevin followed hesitantly. It was cold here in the bowels of the earth, colder than he would expect for a desert summer. The slightest footfall echoed in the dark, and he trod softly where he could. He'd heard the term "silent as the grave" before, but only now understood its meaning. It was a revelation he could have lived without.

At the set of rails, he stopped. There had been a sound, but it was gone now. He tried to think, but couldn't quite recall what it had been. A whisper? He must have imagined it. But Grange had also stopped, staring intently at the hulking shadow, his face unreadable. Unease clenched his stomach. The barracks suddenly seemed a long way off.

As they drew nearer, Kevin saw that Grange hadn't been joshing him: the hulking form was a 'Mech. He expected the dim light would reveal a LoaderMech or even an old MiningMech, but never this.

It was a *Marauder*. Not one of the new-style chassis, but one of the classic GM MAD- series.

It looked pristine—that is, what he could see of it did. Its paint was a flat black that melted into the shadows. No matter what angle he viewed it from, Kevin couldn't quite see it clearly, as if the machine conspired to keep some part of itself hidden. The more he did see, the more his unease gnawed at him. The 'Mech was *wrong*. Its angles were too smooth, its proportions not quite right. It was too sleek, yet its bulk terribly imposing.

Once, when he was a kid, Kevin's father had taken him to a zoo, where some kind of big alien cat was kept in a pit. Looking down at it he felt safe, leaning out over the rail to point, until that cat had looked back at him, and he knew that if he fell in the pit, he would most definitely not be safe. He never forgot the way he felt when those yellow eyes met his, never forgot what would happen if the old rail snapped.

It was the way he felt now, looking at this 'Mech, only there was no rail here.

Grange walked up and put a hand gently on one clawed foot, but withdrew it quickly. He stepped back and looked up at the darkened cockpit. "Hello, you bastard," he said softly. He dropped his gaze to the floor and shook his head.

"Grange, something's..." Kevin could not articulate his question. "Not right."

The old man snorted. "There's a lot of things not right with this *thing*." He put a vile inflection on the word, ascribing it qualities no machine should ever have.

"How did..." Kevin began, but that wasn't the right question. Its answer was insufficient. "Why is it down here?"

"Because it belongs in a hole." Grange walked back into a welcoming pool of light. "I stuck it down here after the War of '39. Back then I'd hoped I'd seen the last of it. Guess you can't bury every secret."

Talking pushed back the strange oppressiveness, and Kevin began to shake off his unease. He had a great many questions, each one crying for an answer, each answer undoubtedly leading to another question. There was a story behind this 'Mech, no doubt, but here, in this place, Kevin questioned whether it was a story he wanted to hear.

The *Marauder* leered at him, daring him to come closer, to come into the pit. It taunted him with its *wrongness*. It was nothing he could put his finger on. The reverse-knee joint of the legs, the torso-rotation ring, the particle projection cannons' housings. All looked somehow...off, as if this weren't a genuine *Marauder*, but a copy made by someone who had seen one once, and then recreated it from memory.

That thought formed his next question. "Where did it come from?"

Grange shrugged. "Who knows? It has no serial number. And it hasn't been removed, it's just...not there."

Kevin frowned. Every machine in the Inner Sphere—from toasters to DropShips—had a serial number.

Grange upturned a bucket, sat on it, and lit a cigarette. He sat and smoked, signs that heralded one of his trademark stories. Kevin had been subjected to more than one of these during his time with the unit. Nothing short of an invasion could stop the old man once he got going.

Resigned, he took a seat on the dilapidated rail cart. It groaned a little, but held. He ran over the routine in his mind: smile, nod in the right places, pretend to be interested, add a prompt or two when the old man expected it. He felt the first yawn building in the back of his throat.

"It could've been made anywhere," Grange said. "Kathil, Quentin, Taurus, maybe even somewhere in the Deep Periphery. They never did find all of Amaris' hidden bases, you know." He took a long drag, expelled a cloud of smoke toward the 'Mech. "One thing I do know is that it's very old."

"How can you tell?"

"You get a feel for these sorts of things. This 'Mech has history."

"Real history or spooky-dark-cave history?"

Grange threw him a sharp look, and Kevin raised a hand apologetically. That comment had likely earned him some long, lonely patrol duty, but it was worth it.

"Was right after the Fourth War," Grange said. "I was with the Capellan Dragoons back then. We were headed back to Warren after a pirate-hunting stint along the Taurian border. We had a lot of trouble in that area during the war, especially from Tortuga. The higher-ups eventually sent the Ninth F-C to pay a visit to Lady Death, but until then it was pretty busy.

"We stopped to recharge in an uninhabited system one jump out from Malagrotta. Nothing there but some useless gas giants and an asteroid belt, but we figured since we had a few days, we'd do some exploring." He held up a finger and gave a knowing wink. "Never know when you'll stumble on one of those lost Star League depots." Kevin couldn't help grinning.

"On one of the bigger asteroids, we found that." Grange jerked a disdainful thumb at the *Marauder*. "Was sheer dumb luck. We'd passed that rock inbound and missed it, but on the way out, there it was, plain as can be. Standing out there in the dark, lord of all the nothing it could want. At the time, we thought it was a blessing—brand new *Marauder* and nobody to dispute our salvage rights. So we loaded it onto our *Union* and took off."

Kevin found himself falling into the tale. Grange was a natural storyteller; he had a way with words, inflection, and body language that fixated an audience. The old man might have been saving it all up, rehearsing in his head during the drive out here.

"We should have known right then. It had no markings. No ID number, no unit insignia, nothing. God only knows who left it there, or why.

"No, I know why." His eyes unfocused, and he bowed his head for a moment before continuing.

"And it was so *clean*. Sitting on an asteroid for Kerensky knows how long, and not a speck of dust. A couple of the more religious guys wanted to leave it there, said it must be a shrine to some long-forgotten warrior or something and it would be sacrilegious to take it. Seemed silly at the time, but given what followed..."

Grange reached for a new cigarette. Kevin's lingering unease pointed out how the old man always took care to keep the *Marauder* in sight, never completely turning his back on it. He spared it a glance. The hunched form seemed to be leaning forward, eager to hear its own story.

"I guess the first problem we had was during the jump into Agliana. I don't think anyone on that ship will forget that jump, though we'd all like to and most don't talk about it. Something happened then, in that half second of nothing when you don't exist. I never can recall fully what it was, I just know it left me more scared than I've ever been. I'm not talking 'Clanner bearing down on you with all guns blazing' scared, no sir. I mean the 'shit your pants and curl into a whimpering little ball' kind of terror you only get when you're a little kid, and you're sure the boogeyman's standing right next to your bed."

Kevin raised an eyebrow. The barracks rumor was that the grizzled old sergeant had had his fear surgically removed.

"Sometimes I think I remember what it was. In that second right after you wake up from a nightmare, right before you forget it. But then I do forget, and I can go on living.

"Anyways, I remember coming to, squeezed between my bunk and the deck, with no desire to get out. Everyone on the ship was affected, some more than others. I was one of the lucky ones, one of those able to forget. Tommy—Reg Thompson—well, he wasn't so lucky. Ol' Tommy, he was what you might call 'sensitive.' Seemed to know stuff instinctively. That was downright creepy in itself, but what happened to him still chills my blood like nothing else.

"Right after the jump, Tommy started to scream. It was a mad sound, terrible, like the devil was after him. Hell, maybe he was! Between the screams, all we could get out of him was gibberish. Kept going on about how 'they' weren't dead, just sleeping, and we were opening the door for them to come back. And he made this awful sound, this chanting, over and over again like a prayer. Doc said it was jump psychosis. Said Tommy's mind had forgotten reality, and was fixating on the books he'd been reading."

"Jump psychosis can do that to a man," Kevin said.

"But not all at once, kid. It builds up over time. Tommy had no signs, it was just like a dam burst and washed his mind away. Doc ended up sedating him, but it did no good. Tommy got out and ran, and we had to scour the whole ship for him. You have any idea what it's like having to search an *Invader* and three docked *Union*s for something as small as one man?

"We finally caught up with him on the JumpShip. Somehow he'd managed to slip through the docking collar and into the jump core. That set the ship's captain on edge something fierce. Kept us there another two weeks while he looked for sabotage. Only Tommy wasn't trying to kill us, he was just passing through.

"It was me and two others that finally caught up with him at a maintenance airlock. I'll never forget the look in his eyes as he shut that door. He was completely lucid. Knew exactly what he was doing when he opened that outer hatch and spaced himself. I know it's clichéd, but that's exactly what he did."

"And you blame...this?" Kevin gestured toward the shadow.

"All I know is things like that never happened before it came along, and nothing's happened since I stuck it down here. And you need to be thankful." His piercing blue eyes flashed, and Kevin bowed his head. Questioning the sergeant was always bound to get you some hurt free of charge, and he'd already earned enough today.

"Thompson wasn't the last one it got to. There was a tech—I forget his name, Reynard or Rexban, or something—but he was the bad-attitude kind of guy. Not mean, but miserable. The kind who can find the cow shit in any spring meadow and drag it out and insist you look at it. Nobody liked him, and I still can't say I miss him, but some things you just don't wish on anyone."

Grange lit his third cigarette. Kevin shifted uncomfortably, wondering how much more there was to this story. Outside, that desert sun was growing hotter, and they still had to work in it.

"Anyway, this guy Rexmond, one day he was changing its coolant, bitching up a storm as usual, when he slips on some spill he probably made himself. He ends up covered in coolant with people laughing at him, and of course blames the 'Mech for all his troubles and starts yelling and using all kinds of colorful words against it."

Grange switched to his lecture voice. "Now you know, a gentleman should never call a lady names. Well, that goes doubly so for a bitch.

"In the middle of his tirade, the left PPC discharged. Vaporized him from the waist up, and left us to clean up the rest. I ain't never heard before or since of a PPC firing when a 'Mech is powered down."

"It's impossible," Kevin said. "The capacitors bleed down when the fusion core is in standby, any leftover charge would dissipate harmlessly. It takes a long time to charge a PPC after startup. If he was following protocol, that 'Mech should have been inert, especially if he was changing coolant."

"Well, thanks for the lecture, kid, I didn't know all that," Grange said. "Look, I'm just telling it like it happened. You want to hear this or not?"

The honest answer was no, but the tone that suggested latrine duty was creeping into Grange's voice, so Kevin simply nodded and sat back. "Sorry."

The sergeant collected his thoughts, staring off into the abyssal hole at the cave's far end.

"Then there was Zahi. Zany Zahi, we used to call him. Arabic descent. Guy had a lot of strange ways. Used to get picked on a lot, but he never let it get to him. Had this habit of stopping to pray at inopportune times, like in the middle of a briefing. Pulled a lot of KP duty because of Allah, Zahi did. Never pulled that shit in combat, though, like some have. He had enough good sense not to do that. Whatever craziness he got up to, Zahi left it off the field.

"One day we were out on maneuvers, and Zahi drew the short straw. It had been a couple months since we'd buried Rex, and nothing else had happened. Zahi never had any qualms about piloting the *Marauder*. He always said Allah rode in the jump seat, and nothing could harm him."

Grange spat. "Guess Allah called in sick that day."

"Zahi ended up separated from his lance. The terrain was all hills and valleys, so it was a common occurrence, but you could usually find your way back easily enough. Something went wrong for Zahi that day, something worse than a bad compass.

"We could hear him, but no one could locate him anywhere. He kept saying his sensors were offline and he couldn't see the sun, which was damned odd since it was a clear day. Ol' Colonel Johnstadt got pissed, yelling that this was the reason we needed to do these maneuvers, and what would happen if there was a Liao raid, so he mobilized the whole battalion to go out and find ol' Zany. Standard sweep, search, and rescue. Leave no stone unturned, as it were.

"Zahi's transmission kept growing fainter and fuzzier, like he was getting farther away. The colonel told him to park it and activate his transponder, even told him to get out and shoot up a flare. By now it was getting dark, and even the PBIs were having no luck finding his trail."

Grange said nothing for a while, only rubbed the scalp under his thinning white hair. He looked somehow older than he had when he began this tale. Kevin craned his neck to see the *Marauder* where it crouched, still hunched forward, still listening.

"Anyway," Grange said at last. "Nightfall came, and still no Zahi. The colonel ordered a satellite sweep of the area, but there was too much heavy metal in the hills to see anything useful. Then around midnight, Zahi began to scream.

"Nothing coherent, just a bunch of gibbering in Arabic. HQ looked like someone had dropped a panic bomb on it. They thought he'd run across some pirates that had been hitting worlds in the PDZ. The colonel was yelling at him to calm down and report, but Zahi wouldn't respond to him. Wouldn't, or couldn't.

"Then he stopped yelling, and I wish to god he hadn't. He let out this one long moan, and I tell you, kid, it wasn't anything I'd ever want you to hear. I wake up covered in sweat sometimes, and I may not remember whatever dream caused it, but I remember that moan was a part of it. It's always a part of it, like some kind of sick special effect. It was as if Zahi saw the Devil coming for him, and was watching as Allah gave him away.

"Worst part is, right before the line cut out, I know I heard that same chanting Tommy made, and it was coming from more than one mouth. Zahi wasn't with the unit back then. He never knew Thompson."

A shudder wove down Kevin's body. Grange was getting to him, here alone in the dark. The old man was working him up, but he sensed there was more to it. Grange *had* to tell this story, had to let it out like some twisted catharsis. He'd kept it bottled up for years, all these nights of cold sweats and horrified moans. Kevin was just a handy sounding board, therapy for an old man's inner demons. Just what he needed.

"We found the 'Mech about an hour later, standing right out in the open in a valley that had been swept three times. Cockpit was sealed, and when the PBIs finally climbed up and popped it..." His voice trailed off. Moisture had gathered at the corners of his eyes. "Zahi was gone."

"Gone?" Kevin said. "Gone how?"

"Just gone. We never found a trace of him. The 'Mech was in perfect order, all systems functional. The neurohelmet had even been neatly tucked back on its shelf. And the cockpit safety latches had been sealed from the inside, same as you'd do when you're expecting hostile infantry."

"That's impossible," Kevin found himself saying again.

"Son, haven't you been listening? This thing shits the impossible."

There was a long silence. Grange stared at the ground between his feet, Kevin stared at anything but the looming shadow in the corner.

"So," Kevin said. "Is that when you put it down here?"

"Not just yet. We kept it for a few more years, and there were other events, though none so profound as Zahi's. The colonel kept trying to reassign the thing, but no one wanted it. The legend of a curse had begun. It spent more time sitting in the hangar than anything else. Even the Dispossessed wouldn't take it."

Kevin understood what the word Dispossessed meant, but the true horror of it was lost on him, as he supposed it was on most of his generation. During the devastation of the Succession Wars, BattleMechs became a rare commodity, owned by and passed down through MechWarrior families. The loss of the family 'Mech meant Dispossession, and the loss of everything. No more noble title, no more land grant, no more food on the table for a suddenly destitute family.

Today, 'Mechs were in mass production again, and almost all were property of the state. Dispossession simply meant you were waiting for the next shipment from the quartermaster, instead of living as a desperate grunt, striving to capture a new 'Mech to revive your family's honor. For his part, Kevin was very glad his 'Mech was the property of the Federated Suns.

"Eventually," Grange said, "the colonel ended up taking it for his own ride." He barked a laugh. "That lasted all of one day. He took it out on maneuvers, not to the same place Zahi went, mind you, but off on a different route. Still, he came back two hours late. Had us all worried and ready to start the search party all over again.

"Me and old Jim Mullins were the first to greet him when he dropped down out of the cockpit, pale and looking more tired than I'd ever seen him. 'Get rid of it,' he said to us. No explanation, just, 'I don't care where, I don't care how, just do it.' I've never known someone without fear in my life, but the colonel was as close to it as one can get. Seeing him like that was damn near the end of me. I couldn't let the thing that had done that to him get away with it.

"So I did what he asked. I found the deepest, darkest hole on this world and dropped it in. Took me and Jim three days to haul it out here, fit that door we came through, and blow the main entrance. The colonel didn't want to know about it, and we both swore to never tell a soul. Jim's dead now, so he kept his oath, unlike me."

Grange looked around the cavern, taking in the dim lighting, the rusting rails, the cracked walls. "I never wanted to see this place again. Thirty-five years just doesn't seem like long enough."

"So why bring it back?" Kevin asked. "We're not hurting for 'Mechs. You left it here through the Clan Invasion, the Civil War. What makes you think we need it now?"

The old sergeant sighed. When he spoke again, his voice had turned somber, subdued. "Because this Jihad is a different kind of war. This looks like it could be the one. *The* war. The Word isn't going to stop until the entire Sphere is dead or singing praises to Blake, and they've got the means to do it. And if this is Armageddon, then I want the devil on my side.

"You hear that?" he yelled to the *Marauder.* "We're going to war, you bastard!" His voice echoed long and loud into the depths of the abyss, and Kevin thought the devil just might be able to hear.

"So that's it, then?" he asked. "The Word comes knocking, and you're just going to toss out decades of superstition and drive it out of here?"

"Nope." Grange smiled and pointed a stubby finger. "*You* are."

Kevin sat in silence for a moment. At first, he thought he'd misheard the old man, or that he was joking. But Grange never joked, possibly didn't remember how.

"Me?" he managed.

"You," Grange said. He looked hard at Kevin, a mix of concern and compassion in his eyes. "I didn't drag you down here just because I needed a warm body, I brought you because I need someone I can trust. There are damn few of those on this world, especially ones who can also pilot a 'Mech."

Kevin felt heartened. The largest 'Mech he had ever piloted was the old *Chameleon* he'd learned on back in his academy days. He'd never been sure if he could handle anything larger, never had the chance to try. Grange's faith was like a cool breeze.

"All right." He turned toward the shadow, still hunched forward, still lurking in its pit, inviting him to come in and play. "In a minute."

Grange nodded. "Whenever you're ready."

They sat in silence, Kevin running through things in his head. The old man's story was crap, of course, but there were probably a few grains of truth in it. Maybe some poor tech had gotten killed working on it, that sort of thing happened. Maybe their colonel did tell him to get rid of it for whatever reason, it had to get down here somehow. But that bit about Zahi and his disappearing act? He was sure that part was one of the sergeant's grand embellishments.

Then another thought occurred to him, an even more heartening one. Under the ancient laws of salvage, this 'Mech would belong to him. Well, him and Grange, but somehow he didn't think the old man would contest his ownership. With a 'Mech of his own, especially a *Marauder*, he could command higher pay, better assignments, maybe even a little more prestige and a chance at promotion. Spooky backstory or not, those were some pretty significant balancers toward the positive. They were enough.

A chain ladder hung from the 'Mech's chin. Grange steadied the bottom, and Kevin started up the rungs. The old man had worked him up something fierce with his crazy story and the effects were lingering, but the discipline ingrained by his MechWarrior training overrode any squeamish impulses. His mind fell into routine: this was a BattleMech, and he was a MechWarrior. That was all there was.

He got about halfway up when he glanced up at the cockpit and—

"What is it?" Grange asked.

"I..." Kevin tried to speak, but his throat closed. He swallowed hard. "Thought I saw something."

"Yeah. Maybe." The worn voice was mellow, soothing, understanding. "It's just your imagination, son. There's nothing up there."

Kevin wanted to believe him. Believe that what he thought he had seen was just a reflection, possibly of Grange moving around below. But it hadn't looked much like a reflection. It had looked an awful lot like someone was in the cockpit, someone who had been looking out at him and leaned back out of sight when Kevin's face tilted up.

Grange was directly below him, out of view of the cockpit. "Go on, son."

His palms were slick on the rungs, and he thought how absurd it would be to lose his grip and fall. Right now, it didn't sound so absurd. He wiped his hands on his shirt and took a better grip. The missing weight under his left arm where his sidearm usually sat pulled him down. He hadn't thought he'd need a gun on a trip into the desert. There was a regret for the record books.

He put his hand on the next rung and slowly resumed climbing. His legs felt like someone had attached lead weights to them, and dragging each up to the next step drained him. He kept his gaze fixed unblinking on the cockpit rim, convinced he would see that movement again, and he knew when he did, he'd fall, and Grange had damn well better be up to catching him.

There were four rungs left until he reached the top of the ladder and would have to switch to handholds on the 'Mech's head. Three, and his sweaty palm slipped a little on the chain. Two, and a clinking sound from the ladder below caused his bowels to clench. One, and the blood began to drain from his head.

In a moment, he was going to come up over the rim of the 'Mech's jutting chin and peer directly into the cockpit. What would he see there? Would it be nothing, like all logic said it should be, or would it be more than nothing? Would he find someone there, staring back at him, perhaps long-lost Zahi come to find someone to take his place in limbo?

Of course not. This was ridiculous, nothing was up there. His nerves were on edge from the combination of Grange's story and the atmosphere of the setting he had chosen to tell it in. Kevin gritted his teeth, grabbed a handhold on the side of the head, and pulled himself up.

An instant of doubt hammered at the back of his mind, and for a second he saw, actually saw, a shape in the cockpit seat. Then the spike of adrenaline caused his pupils to dilate, taking in more light, and he saw only an empty command chair on the other side of the glass. Just as he knew he would.

He leaned his face against the cockpit glass, letting its coolness absorb some of the fear. His legs shook dangerously on the last chain rung, and he waited for them to steady before attempting to open the cockpit.

"You all right?" Grange asked.

"I'm good," Kevin said. He took a deep breath and exhaled against the cockpit, fogging the glass. "Just a bit winded."

"Right," Grange mumbled, mostly to himself.

The cockpit was slightly ajar. Kevin inserted his fingers under the lid and lifted. It rose slowly, with a small *hiss* from its hydraulic actuators. He grabbed a handhold and pulled himself up and into the command couch. It was cold, definitely not recently occupied by a warm body. His stupid overactive imagination might get him killed one day, with a heart attack, if nothing else.

The cockpit was spotless. Even the monitor faces, which were normally dust magnets, shone with a polished finish. The smell of stale sweat and burnt electronics that usually accompanied old 'Mechs was absent. Kevin shifted in the seat, and the springs groaned a little under his weight. He found it very comfortable, unlike his battered *Vindicator*'s brick slab.

He ran his hands over the controls, mentally checking off each one as he touched it. Throttle, targeting interlocks, heat gauges—everything was present, and in the right place. He wouldn't even need to adjust anything for his height. The old neurohelmet, one of the bulky kinds that completely covered the head and rested on the shoulders, sat in its cradle above and behind him, as clean as the rest of the instruments. Everything about the cockpit felt...normal.

"How is it?" came a voice from below.

"Everything's fine," Kevin called back.

And it was. He let out a wry snort. There was nothing unusual about this 'Mech, save that it was basically cherry. It was only a machine, a *Marauder*, nothing more. He had let Grange work him all up for nothing, just another one of the sergeant's sick jokes. The old man would be using him as the basis of his next barracks story, the one about how he'd terrified some greenhorn kid into believing in the BoogeyMech.

"We'll need to clear out that deadfall so you can get it out of here. Get the cold-start process running, I'll go back and start setting up the explosives."

Kevin leaned out, saw the wizened face gazing up to him, and gave the thumbs-up. Grange still looked a bit unsure, standing off to the side, well clear of the arm-mounted weapon ports. He waved and headed for the door, and the freedom of sunlight.

Kevin went through the preliminary start-up procedures. Every BattleMech was equipped with voice recognition software and a personalized security code unique to the MechWarrior. Without the proper codes, which Grange hadn't given him, he couldn't bring the machine to full power. He'd have to go into maintenance mode, which techs used to work on 'Mechs in the repair bay. It wouldn't give him full power, and certainly not any weapons, but it would give him enough to move around and walk the *Marauder* out of the cave once they had cleared the entrance.

He began the process to ignite the fusion core, and saw the reactor was already hot and running. All he had to do to gain total control of the machine was fine-tune the neurohelmet to his brainwaves. Kevin chuckled. He'd have to dig into Grange a little bit about that—subtly, of course. The infallible old man had left his cursed 'Mech running all those years ago, instead of shutting it down like any apprentice tech would know to do.

A few more switches, and the cockpit came to life around him. The primary and secondary monitors flickered, the head-up display bloomed into life on the viewscreen and dozens of tiny lights popped on.

"Kindred soul," he heard.

Kevin smiled. "Forget something?" he called, but got no answer. He stood up and looked over the side. The cave was empty. Grange must have said it from the doorway, then ducked out. It was a fair distance away, but the acoustics could carry a voice that far.

Below him, the fusion reactor began to hum as it gained strength. Gentle vibrations wove up through the floor of the cockpit and the command couch. The engine oscillated at an unusual frequency, one that tickled the base of Kevin's skull, right where it met his neck. He leaned back and listened to it for a moment, felt the vibrations as they worked their way up his spine. It was soothing, in a way, almost like getting a massage, but from feathers instead of fingers. He closed his eyes, and vibrant colors blossomed on the back of his eyelids. They were pretty, and wild. Some were unidentifiable, too awesome to describe in frail human words. There were shapes moving in them.

"Hey!"

Kevin jerked up with a gasp. Grange's face peered at him from over the edge of the cockpit, a mixture of anger and relief on the worn features.

"I'm okay," Kevin said, automatically. He didn't feel okay. He felt drained, and very thirsty.

"Didn't you hear me calling you?"

He hadn't. "Sorry, Sarge. I guess I drifted off."

Grange's voice began drifting from the concerned side over to the angry side. "Oh, well, I'm glad you've had a nice nap, Cinderella. Me, I've been out in the hot sun for two hours planting explosives."

Two hours? He couldn't have been out that long. He'd only leaned his head back for a second. Dirt and sweat streaked Grange's face, more than he could have accumulated from just a walk out to the jeep. His brows were creased as he studied Kevin intently.

"Climb out of there," Grange said. "Demolitions aren't my specialty. I want us both outside when I set it off, in case I bring the place down. Not that that would necessarily be a bad thing."

Kevin nodded groggily, barely listening. He took a deep breath and shook his head to clear away some of the cobwebs. He couldn't have been out for so long. It just didn't feel right. He climbed down the chain ladder in a daze, and followed Grange back out to the jeep. The sun shone high in the sky, hammering on them with light and heat.

Kevin grabbed his canteen from the jeep and took a long pull. The water was tepid but sweet as it passed his lips.

"Go easy, kid," Grange said. "That little can has to last you until we get back."

"Yes, sir," Kevin said. He knew Grange was right, but he was so thirsty. The canteen was half empty, but he took one more mouthful before screwing the lid back on.

Grange drove them about half a kilometer away. He shut the jeep off and pulled a small detonator from his shirt pocket.

"Now or never," he said, looking over a Kevin. His thumb hesitated above the trigger.

"What is it?" Kevin asked.

Grange's brow furled. Kevin saw himself reflected in the wraparound visor, saw how his own eyes and cheeks were sunken and dark, and knew what the old man was thinking.

"This was a bad idea." Grange flicked the detonator off and stuffed it back into his pocket. "Damn me. I should have known better. We're going back."

"No, Sarge," Kevin said, as his lethargy melted away. "I'm okay, really. I just nodded off. It's the heat, it gets to me, sucks the energy right outta me, you know."

Grange still looked unsure. He pulled the glasses off to stare at Kevin hard, the kind of stare he gave new recruits who thought they could test him and get away with it.

"Are you joshing me, son? Think real hard, 'cause if you are it'll be more than your career in the can, it'll be your ass. If you're not fit to pilot that 'Mech out of there, you'd better say so right now."

"I'm fine, Sarge," Kevin repeated. He thought he sounded it, too.

Grange lowered his voice. "Is it getting to you?"

"No, Sarge. It..." He thought for a moment. Was it getting to him? Of course not. No matter what the old man thought, that was just a normal 'Mech in there, and Kevin found he wanted it. He wanted it a *lot*.

"There's something off about the engine oscillation. It's, I don't know...wonky. I've read about how certain low-frequency sound waves can mess with your brain, screw up the medulla oblongata or something. They can make you paranoid, make you see things, hear things... All the kind of stuff you told me about earlier. We should have a tech adjust it. I'm thinking that's the whole source of your problems with this 'Mech."

"You just go right on thinking that," Grange muttered, more to himself than to Kevin. He leaned on the steering wheel, staring off at the hill and the dilapidated building.

"I can handle this, Sarge. I'm up to it." He knew it. This was his chance. With that 'Mech in there, he could stand out. He could make a difference, make his superiors take notice of him, and get transferred out of this dump unit and into something more rewarding, somewhere he belonged. Maybe the Crucis

Lancers, or even the Syrtis Fusiliers. Maybe he could finally get an officer's commission. That would be grand, oh yes.

"I have seventy years' experience making bad decisions," Grange said. "I can recognize them when they come along. And I get the feeling this is going to be one of the worst."

He took the detonator from his pocket, flicked it on, and after a moment's hesitation, pressed the button. Even at this distance the sound was enormous, rolling across the desert and returning from nearby hills like the roar of an angry lion, one now free from its pit.

A moment later, the smoke and dust cleared, and a great black hole in the rock revealed the mineshaft, allowing light to penetrate a place it had not touched for almost four decades— and perhaps to one place where it could never go.

KINDRED SOUL

**WARREN CRUCIS MARCH MILITIA HQ
WARREN
CAPELLAN MARCH
FEDERATED SUNS
21 JULY 3074**

"Langstrom."

The name rolled off General Ingram's tongue with a slight hint of disdain and thick with the Outback accent Kevin so detested.

"Sir," Kevin acknowledged, keeping his voice as flat as he could. As a general rule, respect for Ingram ran low in the Warren branch of the Capellan March Militia, and Kevin toed that line heartily. Still, he didn't need the general sensing his dislike, even if it sat on his tongue like vinegar.

In the ten minutes since Kevin had entered this office and sat down, Ingram had not even deigned to look at him. Only now did the general put aside whatever memo had caught his attention to acknowledge Kevin's presence. He leaned back in his chair, staring down his nose at a datapad resting on his ample gut. Kevin assumed it was his request, but it may just as easily been a schedule of the fat fool's social events.

"Request for transfer," Ingram drawled, with a flick of the datapad. "Again. Syrtis Fusiliers this time?"

Kevin nodded curtly. His fourth request for transfer in as many years spelled out why he thought he would be a good match for the Fifth Syrtis Fusiliers. He'd spent days meticulously wording it to hide his loathing for the toilet that was the Warren CMM. That it had gotten as far as fat old Orlando Ingram made his hopes rise. His application for Officer Candidate School a few weeks back had only made it as far as Colonel Eckhart before being rejected.

"Why do you want to leave the Militia?" Ingram asked.

Kevin blinked uneasily. "I've put it all in my request, sir."

"I know what this says." Ingram waved the pad theatrically. "It tells me the whats. I want to know the whys. Why do you think the Militia isn't good enough for you?"

The laundry list of reasons Kevin could have spat out would only earn him a single word, slapped painfully across his carefully prepared request: DENIED. He fumbled for something politic and proper, but came up short. "I just feel like I'm meant for better things. Sir."

"Better things," the general repeated. It came out sounding like *bett-uh thangs*. "I see." He made a notation on the pad. "Better things."

The general scanned through the datapad, eyes flicking back and forth behind his old-fashioned glasses. Kevin found the man harder to read than anticipated. He rarely had trouble making a conversation go his way, but that was usually with the fairer sex, not those in positions of authority. This was a type of relationship he had precious little experience with, so keeping silent until spoken to seemed most prudent. Ingram would have questions, so Kevin would let the general ask, then answer as best he could. That should do just fine.

Unless Ingram took the conversation in a direction Kevin neither expected, nor cared to follow.

"Says here your father was discharged in 3053?"

A shock ran up Kevin's spine, as it always did when someone brought up this most delicate of subjects. "Yes, sir." He hoped Ingram was savvy enough to properly interpret his note of hesitancy as a warning to back off.

"Section Eight. Mental health problems."

Kevin said nothing, only stared at the general, trying to keep the hate out of his eyes. He partially succeeded.

"Don't feel bad, son." Ingram had slipped into a fatherly tone. "A lot of soldiers mustered out after the Invasion. Shell shock ran pretty high. It's—"

"I'm sorry, sir," Kevin said, catching a drop of sweat before it fell in his eye. "I don't see what my father has to do with anything."

Ingram frowned at him. He leaned back, folded his arms over his bulk, and propped two enormous feet on the corner of his desk. Even the soles of his boots shone. "Where's your father now?"

Kevin didn't need to answer; Ingram knew as well as he did. That data file contained Kevin's entire family history. One line would surely read *Father: Lawrence Langstrom, Deceased, suicide, 13 May 3055.* Maybe Ingram wouldn't know the details—the whats or the whys—but Kevin knew. He'd been there, after all. He tried never to think about it, and normally succeeded until someone like this foolish fop of a failed social general brought it up. Resentment roiled in him.

When Kevin didn't answer, Ingram tried a different tack. "I don't suppose these 'better things' of yours involve more action? Is that it?"

Maybe the fool could pick up on things up after all. Pushing his memories back into their closet, Kevin inhaled deeply and called a prepared speech to mind.

"Sir, I've been here almost six years. I've seen combat three times. Twice was against pirates who could barely pilot their 'Mechs. There is no recognition here, no chance to stand out. I want to be an officer someday, sir. I can't do that, I can't *be* that, without a combat record."

"A long combat record doesn't necessarily make a good officer, son."

"But it does help, sir. I feel if I could just do something to stand out, a campaign or two to make myself known—"

"Glory," Ingram said, with a sad nod. "Got yourself a 'Mech, and now you want some shine on it?"

Yes, he had a 'Mech. A *Marauder.* Its blackened silhouette flashed before his eyes, strengthening him.

"Not glory, sir. Experience." This angle could work. "I can't command troops until I know what it's like on the front lines."

"I can tell you what it's like on the front lines," Ingram said. "Seen enough of them. Kathil. An Ting. Blue Hole. Think these are just for show?" He indicated the blossom of bars on his chest. "Bad things happen on those front lines. Things that can damage a man. You don't seem to realize that yet, but your father knew, didn't he?"

Yes, he did, but Kevin wasn't going to give the general the satisfaction of an answer. His uniform itched, up where the collar touched the nape of his neck, and he scratched at it nervously.

"Those kinds of things don't happen here. At least not as much, or as bad. The Militia is safer, son." The general had turned on his fatherly voice again. It sounded patronizing, insulting. "We get raids, we get pirates, we get these damn Taurian terrorists, but we don't get the kinds of thing you see out on those great 'front lines' your holos always go on about." He shook his head again. "You don't know, but if I send you to New Syrtis, you're gonna find out. Word of Blake or Sun-Tzu Liao will teach you."

"I understand that sir, but—"

"I don't think you do," Ingram cut him off. The general adjusted his bulk to face Kevin across his desk, folding huge brown hands over his datapad and staring over the rim of his glasses. "I really don't think you do. You've put some pretty language in here, all kinds of keywords and impressive phrases, but I don't see a single thing that says you understand what it is you're asking for."

"Sir, I'm asking for a chance to further my career. You understand that, don't you?" Kevin waved at the many framed holos lining the wall, Ingram's career record on display. "If I'm ever going to sit where you are one day, I need to get started. I have my own 'Mech, now I need to use it. All I need is your approval, sir. Send me to New Syrtis."

"Just because you've got a personal 'Mech doesn't mean you can choose your assignments."

"I'm not trying to, sir." Kevin felt stonewalled. "All I know is I don't belong here."

Ingram gave him the look of tested patience so often seen on parents enduring the diatribes of a thickheaded child. "Son, maybe you are right where you belong."

Kevin's hope collapsed beneath him. Ingram, like all of them, didn't understand. Or maybe just he didn't care. Here was another social general who didn't care a whit about the needs of his soldiers, only that they stayed in their place, like good little toys. The room grew uncomfortably hot.

"I'm not your son," Kevin growled through gritted teeth.

"What's that?" Ingram's tone carried a forceful steel it had lacked a moment ago.

"Nothing," Kevin said, sitting up to attention. "Sir," he added hastily.

The general glowered at him, beady eyes poking out of his dark face. "I'm sorry, Langstrom, I can't approve your request at this time. We have too many problems—Taurian raids, pirates running around on-world—and I can't afford to be losing any MechWarriors." He tapped the pad a few times, then tossed it aside. "Dismissed."

Kevin stood, and nearly toppled as the blood rushed from his head. He took a deep breath, colors swimming before his eyes. Perhaps it was the surrealism of the head rush that made him ask, or maybe it was just a precursor of the final straw falling a bit early.

"Is it the MechWarrior you need, or just the 'Mech?"

He turned and left the office with that question hanging in the air. There was an old MechWarrior's axiom from Ingram's glory days—*Life is cheap, BattleMechs aren't*. Kevin thought the general was just the kind of person to carry that old baggage into this new age of manufacturing power. A MechWarrior who didn't hang on Ingram's party line might find themself replaced, but a BattleMech was like gold.

Heart pounding with useless rage, Kevin headed almost unconsciously to the hangar, where his 'Mech waited. *His* 'Mech. Now there was a thought to calm his roiling nerves. Though family 'Mechs had been the norm a generation or two ago, few MechWarriors laid claim to own their machines these days. Thanks to a certain rotten old sergeant, Kevin was among them. He commanded higher pay than his peers—although much of it went into maintenance and buying his own ammo—and he should have commanded greater respect, but that last bit hadn't come yet.

Thoughts of Ingram were shunted aside as he remembered the day six months earlier, when his life had changed. He and old Grange, driving deep into the Padishan Flats to an old, abandoned mine, and the miracle hidden within. By the ancient salvage laws, it belonged to Grange, but the old man had some silly ideas about the 'Mech and didn't want it. Instead, he'd gifted it to Kevin, filling out all the proper paperwork and getting the lawyers to sign off on it.

And that should have been the beginning of a better life for MechWarrior Corporal Kevin Langstrom. Except for old Grange and his silly ideas. Less than a week after he'd walked the 'Mech out of the desert and into the Warren CMM garrison, Kevin began to notice a difference in his treatment, and it wasn't one of respect. He'd never been the most popular guy in the unit, but now he'd become a pariah.

He didn't have to ask where this behavior came from. Despite vowing he wouldn't repeat the tale he'd told Kevin in the bowels of the earth, Grange had surely spread it. Spread it wide and far. Maybe he hadn't meant to, maybe he'd just gotten drunk and told it to one or two curious people he thought he could trust, but it had gotten around as quickly as an off-world virus. Doubtless it had morphed and mutated and grown more terrifying with each retelling until it little resembled Grange's original version, which had been scary enough as it was. Kevin didn't need to hear it again, nor any of its mutant offspring. Somehow, he was living it. Where he'd been lonely in the unit before, now he was truly alone.

But he had his 'Mech. He smiled as he entered the hangar. A tingle worked up his spine, settling between his shoulder blades like the point of a knife. He'd first felt it in the blackness beneath the earth, when it had been fear, brought on by a foolish old man's tales of gore. In the last six months it had morphed into something better: excitement, anticipation, longing. Another few steps would bring it into view. Already the barrel of the dorsal autocannon was visible, poking forward into the bay, black as night.

Kevin's heart rose as more of it slid into view. Clawed feet that tore the earth in great chunks; chin-mounted antenna sticking out like poison spines; reverse-canted legs and hunched-over body; the silhouette that had ushered in a new era in BattleMech manufacturing so many centuries ago. It was, in a simple word, a *Marauder*...but not just any *Marauder*. This was Grange's legendary *Marauder*. The *Marauder* that had called a dark cave and a lonely, forbidding planetoid home. The *Marauder* that had killed only its own. Kevin's *Marauder*.

It was a *Marauder*, but...somehow it wasn't. It did not quite match the images in ComStar's technical readouts. It was close enough to pass the untrained eye, but for MechWarriors whose lives depended on studying these machines of war, the differences stood out. Some said it was bulkier, its edges sharper. The autocannon rotator ring was wrong, the hip joint too wide. No consensus of its oddities had been reached, but the one thing everyone agreed on was that it looked meaner than your average *Marauder*. No, not meaner. The word they used most often was *sinister*. The 'Mech looked sly, like a predator that feigned innocence before pouncing.

As he stepped into the *Marauder*'s pooled shadow, Kevin laughed at their fear. Such superstitions were a symptom of being raised in the uneducated Outback. They believed Grange's story just as completely as they believed in the Vandenburg White Wings and the disappearing battleship of Merope. So what if it was different? It was still only a 'Mech.

He climbed up to the cockpit and settled into the command couch. For a few moments he simply sat there, staring unseeing at the controls while Ingram's face laughed in his memory.

"Looks like we'll be here a bit longer," he grumbled to his dark monitor.

Kevin leaned his head back and shut his eyes. Napping in the cockpit had become a semi-regular habit. The *Marauder* had a peculiarity in its engine-oscillation frequency that manifested as a barely felt vibration in the command couch. It massaged his spinal column, tickled the back of his brain. The overall effect was soothing. It produced an impressive array of lights behind his eyes and sparked dreams of incredible intensity, though it occasionally left him feeling drained, like he'd run one of Grange's calisthenics courses in double time.

He pushed aside the tempting whisper; there was work to do. For weeks, he'd felt a strain in the 'Mech's left leg, and was at a loss to diagnose it. After a little exertion, it developed a limp that lasted until he powered down. Lubricant had to be the problem. He'd tried every available blend of oils and dry lubes, no matter how esoteric and hard to come by, but none of them worked. It needed something else besides standard machine-shop goop, but he had no idea what. There was nothing left for it but to strip down the leg—tear off the armor and inspect each myomer coil individually. It would be a tough, long project, but time was something he had. It wasn't like he'd be packing for New Syrtis any time soon.

As he worked at dismounting access panels and even whole armor plates, his conversation with Ingram replayed over and over in his head. Things he should have said and proper ways to answer the general's questions came into his mind, and Kevin found himself muttering them under his breath. These eventually morphed into fantasies of punishing Ingram, both now and in a nebulous future where Lord Langstrom held a beaten and humiliated Ingram in his dungeon. Such fantasies were dangerous, but it wasn't like he could help them. They buzzed deep in his mind like a truth waiting to be paroled.

The more armor he removed, the more he was amazed at the space inside the leg. Most 'Mech limbs only allowed enough clearance for the myomers to expand and contract comfortably, but the inside of the *Marauder*'s leg was downright roomy. He could climb inside and stand in the space between the armor and the bones. It was tight, but manageable. This would doubtless rate high on the weirdness scale if he ever told the techs about it, but Kevin simply used it to his advantage, loosening plates from the inside for faster removal.

A shadow blocked out his light. Looking out, Kevin saw Dean Ipswich grinning down at him. He relaxed the irritated grip on his wrench. Ipswich was a man on friendly terms, if not a friend. There were precious few of those in Kevin's life these days, and he didn't need to lose any via accidental bludgeoning.

Dean was a lifer, continuing his family's long tradition serving the Capellan March Militia. He had a reverence for the unit Kevin could never understand, yet he never lorded it over anyone. He simply loved to be where he was and do what he was doing, and that kind of person never wanted for happiness.

Everyone was friends with Dean Ipswich. Upon meeting him, no one could ever consider having it any other way.

"How ya doin', Kev?" Ipswich's smile was genuine but hesitant, as if he didn't know whether it would be welcome or not.

"All right, I suppose." Kevin slid out of the leg. "You?"

"Good," Ipswich nodded. His voice held a higher pitch than normal, and his eyes shifted, not meeting Kevin's for more than a second at a time. "You're a hard man to get a hold of these days, without one of these." Dean held up a pry bar, then mimed shoving it between Kevin and the 'Mech and strained. "This'll work, I know it!"

Despite himself, Kevin smiled.

Dean dropped the bar with an exaggerated sigh. "Worth a try. C'mon, Kev, you've had your head stuck in this thing for months. You know you need air and food and stuff, right?"

"Lots of work to do," Kevin mumbled. "It's been sitting a long time. Sand's gotten all into it—actuators, myomer bundles, wiring. It all needs servicing."

"Still haven't been able to hire a tech, huh?"

Kevin shook his head. Personal 'Mechs were traditionally serviced by personal techs, and family BattleMechs were backed up by rich family estates. Kevin's lack of both smarted in more than one way.

Dean grinned. "Grab one of the apprentices and chain them to the leg. Get 'em some tools, give 'em some beer once a day, they'll be fine."

The light attempt at humor may have succeeded, if Kevin didn't already know exactly what the tech pool thought of his *Marauder*. They hated it. "Laid out all wrong" is how one senior tech put it after a quick examination. "Parts where they shouldn't be, others missing outright... The damn thing shouldn't even run at all!" Then Grange's story had begun to circulate. Techs who were already skittish about the 'Mech became downright terrified, even openly hostile at the prospect of working on it. Some of them might die of heart failure at the idea of being chained to it.

"You've been working too hard, Kev," Ipswich was saying. "You seen a mirror lately? You look like hell, man."

Reflexively, Kevin glanced at the polished surface of his tool cabinet. The man standing beside the mirrored Ipswich was familiar, but somehow alien. Sure, his clothes fit the same, and he had the same sandy-blond hair and brown eyes the ladies at the university had melted in, but there was a tightness about those eyes now, a shadow over the brow. He looked like a man who hadn't slept in the week after finding out his family had died.

"Just a little tired," Kevin said. "And maybe a bit stressed. The meeting with the general didn't go well."

"Sorry to hear that," Dean said, and he really sounded like he meant it. "What you need is a good night out. It's been months since you came out with us."

Kevin furrowed his brow, trying to remember. Had it been that long? He supposed it had. He had a vague memory of being at a club or a bar with Ipswich and a couple others, of dancing with a girl, of maybe getting hit by someone. When was that? January? No. October? Maybe it was.

"Tonight, 2100 hours," Ipswich said. "Me, Anders, some of the other guys. And you. Life is a series of choices, my friend. You can choose a fun night with us, or you can choose a greasy night alone."

Choices. Kevin tried to avoid them when he could. Lately he never seemed to make the right one.

Dean swatted the *Marauder*'s clawed foot. It was one of the few times Kevin had seen anyone else touch it. "Forget this thing," he said. "There's a beer out there with your name on it, and maybe even a Mechbunny to go with it. All you've got to do is come claim 'em." He gave the charming, irresistible smile that always cheered his fellows.

Part of Kevin wanted to accept, but that part seemed to be calling from inside a locked room, one he had lost the key to. A Mechbunny would be nice, even a Warren Mechbunny. She'd certainly be softer and warmer and maybe even smell better than a *Marauder*, but she didn't come with the same...satisfaction. Sleeping next to her wouldn't yield the same dreams.

Dean slapped Kevin on the shoulder, making him start. "2100 hours, that's eight hours from now. Plenty of time to put this thing back together. Don't be late!" Concern crossed his handsome face. "You've got friends here, Kev—even if you pretend not to see them."

Kevin managed a weak smile, and Dean left, calling out to someone on his way.

With a sigh, Kevin picked up his tools again. Dean's last words resonated as he worked, but their truth felt questionable. If he had friends, where were they? Why did he feel so abandoned? There might be an answer someplace where there was no black shadow over his life.

The next time a literal shadow fell over him, it wasn't as pleasant. "Hey, Langstrom!"

Kevin hated that voice. High pitched, nasal, and Outback typical, it belonged to Byron Dylan, a man of particular distaste. Byron was a short man, and had a short man's attitude. He claimed a distant relation to the Davion family, which few believed, but he did pilot the newest 'Mech in the battalion, so maybe there was some truth to it.

"Are you ever gonna put that piece of crap back together?" Byron said.

"When I'm finished." Kevin didn't turn around, just continued heating frozen bolts with a butane torch. Maybe if Kevin ignored him, he'd go away.

Nope, too much to ask. Ignoring a bully never worked.

"Hell, you ain't never gonna be finished." Kevin could hear the cruel smile in Byron's voice. "Your grandchildren are gonna be working on that thing."

Kevin sighed. He raised the torch and swung to face his visitor.

"Hey, watch it!" Byron yelled, raising his hands against the blue flame.

Kevin looked at him for a second, trying hard to keep his evil grin in check as he dialed the torch down. "Sorry."

Byron took a step closer. "I oughta report you for safety—"

"Do you want something, Byron?"

The little man's lips worked for a second below his blazing eyes. He looked like he wanted to hit Kevin, and if he'd been accompanied by his usual gang of thugs, he might have.

"Just be more careful," Byron muttered, backing off.

They'd had many exchanges like this over the past two years, ever since Byron had come to the Militia. His classic Napoleon complex brought him into conflict with just about everyone, but his supposed family relations and unabashed brownnosing of officers kept him out of the disciplinary action pool. Those connections hadn't prevented him from earning the nickname of Little Napoleon, which he violently hated. And that was the point.

"Heard you applied for OCS," Byron said, dropping into a more civil tone.

More bitterness. "How'd you know about that?"

"A man hears things. Especially an informed man."

Of course, Kevin thought. Byron was so informed, he was just now bringing up a failure over a week old. It would probably take him even longer to hear about today's rejection of his transfer request, then he'd happily poke that wound too.

"So, how'd it go?" Byron sneered. "C'mon, I want to know if you're going to make leftenant before me." He said the last with a little smile, as if it were a friendly competition between them.

Despite his efforts to control it, Kevin's blood pressure rose. If Byron knew about his application, then he was informed enough to know its results.

"Don't worry," he said, returning to his work. "The game's still on." He wanted the fool to go away, before the urge to turn his torch back on became too strong.

"Yeah, I figured as much," Byron drawled, a bit of his cockiness coming back. "It's all about who you know, Kevin old buddy, and you just don't know the right people. My evaluation is tomorrow morning, and I've got a good feeling about it. This time next year, I may be wearing a new set of bars on my shoulders. Then it will formally be 'I lead, you follow.'"

That was one of Little Napoleon's favorite sayings. Although it only applied to his four or five cronies, Byron tried to impress it on everyone he thought he outranked, and even a few of the weaker NCOs. Rumor was he'd once pulled that line on Grange, an event that had led to him spending a month garrisoning the southern polar listening station.

"One can dream," Kevin said.

Petty anger slipped back into Byron's voice. "You know, you're not better than the rest of us, Langstrom, no matter what you seem to think." He took a few steps forward, and suddenly found himself in the pool of dark cast by the *Marauder*. He twitched as if he'd stepped on a live wire, and jumped back. Kevin smelled Grange's story in the air again, but this time it amused him.

Byron waved a weak hand at the 'Mech. "You need to get rid of this thing. It's never gonna be worth it. It's just a cheap pile of scrap." He looked over his shoulder at the 'Mech across the way, his *Centurion*, with the asinine name *Bucket of Love* slapped on its chest. "And turn it away. I don't like it looking at my 'Mech like that."

"Sure," Kevin said. "Whatever you say."

"I'm serious! It looks nasty, like a sick animal. I don't want any of that rubbing off on *Bucket*."

"Goodbye, Byron," Kevin said. He began cranking again, the clatter drowning out any reply Byron may have made. Kevin was sure he'd made one, as Byron's ego always demanded the last word, but Kevin was done with him.

Delving back into the bundles of myomer and steel bones, Kevin pushed Little Napoleon and all other irritating things from his mind. Working was cathartic, and he needed it today. Better to put that angry energy to use, rather than sulk or drown his sorrows in a bottle. He tore down the lower leg bundle by bundle, cleaning and running a current through each to test flexibility. Each tested fully functional. All of them worked fine individually, but when assembled they failed to cooperate.

"What do you need?" Kevin asked the darkened cockpit. "How am I supposed to know?"

No answer, but he'd expected none.

Outside, darkness had fallen. His chronometer read 2232. Afternoon and evening had passed him right by. He'd never even felt hungry. With a pang, he remembered Dean's invitation. An ache irritated the back of his head. Ipswich would get over it. In the meantime, Kevin had work to do.

Sixteen hours later, Kevin slipped into the briefing room with a sigh of relief. He wasn't late, though he was cutting it close. Hushed murmuring and the occasional bout of laughter floated across the room, buoyed by the underlying tension. Emergency briefings were called such for a reason, and few were ever eager to learn it.

He spotted an open chair and made for it, groaning silently when he reached it. Slouched next to the seat, like an accusation, was Grange. Legs stretched out in front, feet crossed, head lowered, and arms folded across his chest, this was his angry posture, the one he assumed when things weren't going his way and there wasn't a damn thing he could do about it. Kevin glanced around, hoping for another empty chair, but found only the one on Grange's other side.

Resigned, he sat down as timidly as if he were planting his backside on a landmine. He'd been avoiding the sergeant since this unwelcome rift had formed between them. They had shared, if not a friendship, at least a camaraderie and a mutual respect, but over the past few months the camaraderie had eroded, and the respect was sliding along with it.

It was, of course, the 'Mech. *His* 'Mech. Grange distrusted it even more than the other 'Mech jocks. Kevin wondered how much of his own story the old man believed. All of it? He distrusted the 'Mech, and now he distrusted Kevin for spending so much time with it. Kevin missed the old man's grudging approval, but not so much that he'd throw out his future because Grange couldn't keep his superstitions in line. Nothing had occurred to validate those tales of the 'Mech's dark side. No deaths, no strange disappearances, no injuries. He had a nagging suspicion the damn fool thought the machine was biding its time, waiting for him to drop his guard before it acted.

Grange favored him with a glower, taking in his grungy overalls, his grease-stained hands. "Working on it again." It wasn't a question.

"Left leg's not pulling its weight." Kevin kept his tone neutral. "I'm running a diagnostic."

He didn't want to let the old man know how badly he'd lost track of time. The announcement came forty minutes ago, and Kevin figured he'd have just enough time to finish the scan he was doing and get cleaned up. When the scan finished, he'd decided to test the next myomer bundle. Then the next. There was a moment of confusion when he noticed he was alone in the 'Mech bay, then he remembered with a jolt where he was supposed to be, and had only five minutes to get there or face a tardiness review.

"Was a time you used to go out when your buddies asked." Grange nodded across the room, where Dean Ipswich sat with some friends. Dean threw Kevin a wave when he noticed them looking, but it was a sad gesture, more polite than friendly. How'd Grange know Dean had invited him out last night? Had he only asked on Grange's insistence?

This wasn't a line of thought Kevin wanted to continue. He looked around at the gathered troops. "I take it this is about more than just our visiting pirates?"

In the last few weeks, a small band of pirates had taken a liking to Warren. Their first victim was the city of Iridium, about 300 kilometers from the garrison, where they'd robbed a few banks and turned the local law enforcement officers into martyrs. Since then, they'd struck three more cities along the river. Always the same MO: hit the banks, crush the police forces, and fade back into the countryside before the Militia could respond. At least they only seemed to be after money instead of military supplies or slaves.

"Not likely," Grange said. "Full-regiment briefings like this only occur for one reason. And it's not one I like."

A knot built in Kevin's stomach. He knew what the old man was thinking, knew he was probably right.

A moment later, Colonel Jonathan Eckhart, commander of the Militia's BattleMech regiment, entered the room and strode to the podium. Talk was replaced by the sound of chairs scraping as every soldier stood and saluted. Though General Ingram was the ranking officer on-world, all planetary operations were delegated to Colonel Eckhart. Orders went out under his signature first, the general's second. As far as most were concerned, Eckhart was their only commander.

"At ease," the colonel said, waving them back to their seats. "We've got little time, so I'll make this brief. Three hours ago, we picked up an emergence wave at a pirate point less than a day away. Five JumpShips, all fully loaded. Their transponders are off, and the ships have refused all hails. I'm sure most of you can guess what comes next."

Kevin exchanged a glance with Grange, and the old man mouthed one word: "*Cows.*"

The colonel validated him. "Long-range sensors have confirmed our visitors as a Taurian invasion force."

Murmuring swept the room. The colonel let it continue for a moment, then held up his hands for silence. "The Taurians have hit our PDZ hard lately. It was only a matter of time before they came to Warren. They've justified this invasion by blaming us for the bombardment of Samantha on Taurus, and the loss of so many lives. They refuse to listen to reason, and have tossed diplomacy to the wind. We've been spread out across the PDZ fighting them off for a while now, and it's beginning to show. We're looking at less than two combined-arms regiments defending Warren, and judging by the inbound force, they've sent at least that much to take it from us. We're going to hold as long as we can. I've already sent a message to New Syrtis informing them of our situation and asking for immediate reinforcement. With the war against the Blakists being what it is and the Capellans still rattling sabers, I don't know what kind of response we'll get."

A woman in the third row shot up her hand. "Sir, is it true the Taurians are using nukes?"

Eckhart leaned heavily on his podium. His face, usually a mask of seriousness, was downright grave. "Affirmative."

Another round of urgent whispering filled the room. Grange bowed his head.

"Weapons of mass destruction were deployed against Militia units on Midale," the colonel said. "Reports suggest the Taurians bit off more than they could chew, and a nuke was their only hope for victory."

"They had to resort to that to beat us?" someone shouted. It was Byron. A chorus of angry jeers rose up. Byron's cronies began rousing chant of "Nuke them back!"

"We will *not* be doing that!" Eckhart hushed the crowd with a stern glower. "We are not the Fifth FedCom. We will abide by the rules of warfare, even if our enemies don't. Not sinking to their level is what makes us better. It's what makes us Sons of the Suns."

Shame silenced the loudmouths in the room. Eckhart went on for a few more minutes, extolling the virtues of the Suns over the Taurians, the Capellans, and every other nation not headed by someone named Davion. It was textbook rabble-rousing, designed to boost morale in the face of impending battle. Kevin tuned most of it out, answering with only a half-hearted "Yes, sir!" when it was required.

"So, that's our situation," the colonel concluded. "You have sixteen hours before we deploy. Get your machines in order, get fed, and get rested. Dismissed!" He saluted, and walked off the stage.

The room emptied slowly, with much jostling in the crowded aisles. Grange stayed in his seat, head still bowed. He hated crowds, and would stay put until it filtered out. Though he didn't know why, Kevin stayed with him. It was like sitting beside a loved one before the scars of a bitter argument had healed.

"I don't get this," Kevin finally said. "Do the Taurians really think we dropped an asteroid on their planet?"

"Apparently," Grange said. It was one of his trademark one-word answers, but the fact it wasn't a trademark grunt was encouraging.

"C'mon, who the hell can do that? It's like they look for things to blame on the Suns. Next it'll be a plague or famine that's somehow our fault. When's the last time we actually attacked them? I mean *really* attacked, not just raided."

"Reunification War. Five centuries or so."

"Five hundred years?" Kevin sighed. The Taurians' logic simply failed to register with him. "And now they want to come take Warren. Why?"

"Because it used to be theirs. Most of these local worlds used to be theirs, and they want to come liberate their people. They've been itching for more since they took the Pleiades. Warren's probably been on their list for years."

"Warren was theirs for a few years, then ours for the next five centuries, and they still think it's theirs? Do they think the people actually want them here?"

"They're Periphery, kid. Don't ascribe to them qualities they lack, such as intelligence or common sense."

Kevin had nothing to say to that. He sat back, and the longest conversation they'd had in months came to an end. The room had nearly cleared out.

Grange stood and stretched, his neck cracking loudly. "You'd better go get your machine back together."

"I'll need some help," Kevin said, thinking of the stack of armor plates sitting beside the *Marauder*'s naked leg.

"If you can find it, take it." With that, the older man turned and walked off.

Kevin glared at his back. Grange had the authority to order a tech to help him put the *Marauder* back together, and a direct order was the only way he'd get it.

Sure enough, the entire tech pool was otherwise occupied. They worked in gangs, crawling down the line of 'Mechs, topping off ammo and coolant, and replacing any damaged armor plates. Thirty men working efficiently could service a 'Mech battalion in a surprisingly short time, and before Kevin had reattached the armor plating on the inward side of the *Marauder*'s leg, they'd checked out every other 'Mech in the hangar. He resentfully watched them leave, none of them even bothering to ask if he needed help. Growing more tired and bitter by the second, he worked on.

A short time later, Kevin sensed eyes on him, and turned to find Grange standing nearby. He didn't miss how the sergeant carefully kept out of the arc of the *Marauder*'s weapons.

"You could lend a hand," Kevin said, glaring down from his scaffolding.

"No, I can't." Grange crossed his arms over the scaffold, gazing upward. "I just can't."

Kevin repressed his anger. "Then what do you want?"

"Just checking on you. Seeing if you're...okay."

"And what the hell's that supposed to mean?"

"You haven't noticed that you're a bit twitchy lately?"

"Maybe," Kevin grunted.

"I think you should go see the doc before it becomes a problem."

Kevin ran a hand through his hair. "I don't need my head shrunk, I just need some rest."

Grange nodded, but not in agreement. He cast the *Marauder* a dour glare, his thoughts written on his face.

"I don't get you, Sarge." Kevin's brows knitted together. "If you're so scared of this thing, then why'd you want to bring it back? Why didn't you just leave it down in that cave?" *Why put me through this?*

Grange never broke his steady, analytical gaze. "The Word, the Taurians. We're in more trouble now than ever. This isn't like the Clans. It's not happening around stars we can't even see. This is home, and the war's coming here. We need all the help we can get, even if I'd rather not have it."

"Bullshit—that isn't it!" Kevin shouted. "You like telling that damn story. You can't resist an audience! Let 'em give you attention and buy you a drink or two, and you'll tell 'em anything. You love it. Don't deny it, you know you do!"

The old sergeant just stared at him unblinking, piercing him with those steel-gray eyes. Under other circumstances, Kevin knew he'd be looking at months of punishment detail for his diatribe, but Grange was different where the *Marauder* was concerned.

"I thought you respected me," Kevin said. "Sometimes—I even thought we were friends."

"We still would be." Grange spoke so softly his words were almost lost on the cold desert breeze flowing through the bay. "But one of us has forgotten how."

He walked off, leaving Kevin stricken.

Filled with unexpected hollowness, he returned to the *Marauder*'s exposed, balky myomers. They still screamed for lubricant, but they'd just have to wait. If he had to go into battle tomorrow limping, then so be it. The Cows could laugh, but they'd still die.

The bay grew quieter as the darkness deepened. Kevin alternated working with long bouts of simply staring at the myomers, Grange's last words scraping along his nerves. Some time later, footsteps echoed through the empty hangar, and Kevin guiltily grabbed his wrench and set back to work. With his luck, it was Eckhart coming to scream at him.

"How ya doing, baby?" Kevin glanced over his shoulder and saw Little Napoleon gazing lovingly up at his *Bucket of Love.* "Ready to go tomorrow? I knew you'd be. We'll kick some Taurian butt, you and me." He kissed his palm and smacked it against the *Centurion's* foot. "Sleep tight, baby."

Kevin groaned. Eckhart would have been preferable to enduring Byron making love to a BattleMech. He tried to feign invisibility or melt into the scaffolding so the little fool wouldn't see him and—

"Hey, Langstrom!"

Damn it.

Byron sauntered over, grinning with self-important smugness. "Have you heard the good news?"

"The Taurians are leaving?" Leaving like he wished Byron would.

"Better." Little Napoleon preened like a peacock. "My application to OCS was approved. I'll be shipping off right after we get rid of the Cows."

"You're kidding." Kevin's gut felt like it had been lanced. Ingram and Eckhart were sending this little asshole to become an officer? While he was left to rot here? What the hell was wrong with them? He gripped his wrench so tightly his hand ached.

Byron scowled. "Y'know, I don't think I like your tone, Langstrom. I'm not going to tolerate that when I'm wearing leftenant's bars. You'd better learn to start treating me with more respect."

"Better work on earning it, then." Kevin rubbed the back of his head, which had begun to throb. "I have work to do, *leftenant,* so if you'll excuse me..."

He went back to tightening the bottom-most armor plate, twisting the bolts as if each were Byron's smug face.

The little man never knew when to let things go. "I thought I told you to turn this thing away," Byron spat. "I hate the way it looks at me."

"It's just a machine, you moron!" Kevin's weariness and irritation put him in no mood for idiotic superstitions.

Byron turned scarlet. "What'd I just tell you, Langstrom? You've got no respect for anyone but yourself. You know who you are? You know who you really are? Nobody, that's who! You're just a stuck-up little nobody, with your prissy, off-world arrogance."

Hot blood pounded in Kevin's ears. "Shut up," he growled, tears pooling in the corners of his eyes.

No, the little man never knew when to stop. "Think you're big 'cause you have your own 'Mech? Well what else do you have? Nothing, that's what. No friends, no future. No one here likes you, no one's gonna miss you when you're gone. And believe me, you'll be gone one day! One day soon, if I can help it."

"Shut up!"

"I'll have you cashiered out of here, or maybe even court-martialed, and this heap of trash will be sent to the scrapyard where it belongs. It'll rot, and so will you, down in some deep, dark hole!"

"SHUT UP!" Kevin roared. The throbbing in the back of his head burst forward, shunting his conscience into a cubbyhole. Rage like he'd never known tore through him, overriding everything but the need for an outlet. And it had one.

Kevin spun around, raising the wrench high, registering the sudden terror on Byron's face as he realized he'd just pressed past the boundaries of too far. Idiot he may be, but Byron still possessed a MechWarrior's sharp reflexes, and the blow meant for his head crashed onto his collarbone. There was a muffled *crack*, and Byron crumpled with an agonized shriek.

Kevin brought the wrench up again. Byron raised his right arm defensively, his left hanging useless at his side.

"Don't!" he shrieked in a high, girlish voice. "Kevin, don't! Ah, god, my arm!"

The wrench came down, powered by rage and adrenaline. *Whack!*

Byron screamed again, but Kevin didn't hear. All he heard was the rushing, and the whispering tickle that encouraged him, told him he was right. Over and over he brought the wrench down, a sadistic drummer banging his canvas.

"I—" *Whack!* "—told you—" *Whack!* "—to—" *Whack!* "—shut up—" *Whack!* "—you—" *Whack!* "—little—" *Whack!* "—bastard!" *Crunch!*

A jet of fluid sprayed into Kevin's eye. It didn't shock him, but it made him pause. Panting, he wiped his face with a wrist that came away red. Byron Dylan lay in a heap. Little Napoleon had found, if not his Waterloo, certainly his road to Moscow. Kevin felt his rage drain away, taking something with it he might never get back. He didn't know if he missed it or not. A solid block of nothing filled every centimeter of him.

The pile of Byron leaking crimson onto the floor presented a problem. It would have to go away. A hose would take care of most of it, but the parts that couldn't be washed away needed attention. A gleeful voice in the back of his mind whispered a solution. Kevin regarded the *Marauder*'s open leg, with its unusually large space between armor and myomer. It needed a different kind of lubricant, so it would get one. One rich in iron.

Kevin worked with focused diligence, sliding the interlocking plates into position one by one, fastening their bolts and ensuring the environmental sealing was in place. The topmost plate filled a gap a half-meter wide. As he set it into place, Kevin thought he heard a low, forlorn moan drift from the gap. He listened for a moment, thinking there might be words in its low warbling, then got back to work. He dismissed the sound as just his imagination, just like he must be imagining that irregular tapping. No matter, it would stop eventually.

Kevin slept in the *Marauder*'s cockpit that night. Partly to keep an eye out for people in the hangar, and partly for the dreams. Mostly for the dreams. He expected to feel a bit of regret over what he'd done to Byron, a bit of shame to interrupt his sleep, but there was nothing. He had merely silenced an incessant pest, like stepping on a bug. No one else would see it that way, of course, but no one else had to know. People went AWOL occasionally, especially cowards on the eve of battle. That would be the natural supposition, and Kevin certainly wouldn't discourage it.

So he slept, and he dreamed. That wonderful tickling sensation, what he liked to think of as the 'Mech's engine-oscillation frequency, started the minute he shut his eyes, soft fingers dancing on the nape of his neck. Then the shapes, and the colors. Oh, the colors! The spectrum of human vision in its limited, blinkered state could not cope. The eyes made poor utensils, unable to pick up so much of what the brain can comprehend. Colors unheard of danced in his mind, colors he named—for lack of a proper frame of reference—infra-green, ultra-blue, and sideways red.

And in them marched the shapes. Persons, though not people, met him and shook his hand. Places formed from the random images, places of power. He stood on a mesa of blackest pink and looked down into the sky. A person with the faces of Ipswich, his sister, and a Mechbunny he'd once bedded stood near him, encouraging him to jump, while another who looked like Ingram and his father told him not to.

He jumped. He fell for kilometers through the nothing, and when he landed, he hit solid earth with both feet. Both black, clawed feet, and his arms ended not in hands, but in pods that dealt lightning and death. And there he waited, until a dull, ugly ball descended from the heavens, and out came a person with one face and two gray eyes, a person who was his enemy.

Sound. Sound tore away the dreams, and they faded as they always did into half-remembered nonsense. A blaring klaxon echoed throughout the base. Kevin wiped his eyes and drew a deep breath. He heard that sound every Saturday during drills, accompanied by the announcement that it was only a test. But this was not Saturday morning, and there was no flat, toneless voice to issue reassurances. This was Thursday, and the Bull had come back from the pasture.

In moments, the bay swarmed with activity. Orders were shouted, and BattleMechs lumbered out to meet their equals on the field of war. Refreshed, Kevin felt eager to go. At last would come combat. At last, a chance to prove himself a warrior, and not just a killer. He was ready, and so was the *Marauder.* He didn't remember powering it up, but he must have at some point in the night, at some point during the dreams.

Across from him, *Bucket of Love* stood unmoving. It would not take the field that day. Would it wonder where its pilot was? Would it miss him? Of course not, it was only a machine.

OUTSIDE COBALT
WARREN
CAPELLAN MARCH
FEDERATED SUNS
29 JULY 3074

Barely more than a few crossed streets and a rail line, the town of Cobalt sat within the maze of crumbling buttes and mesas on the outskirts of the Padishan Flats. Its existence was dependent on the mines dotting the region, and when they finally petered out, Cobalt would be left to parch in the desert sun like so many of its neighbors. Until then, it was the largest mining town in these badlands, and as such it held strategic importance. Kevin had no idea what that meant, but apparently the Taurians did, since they'd dispatched a company to take it.

The Cows had arrived at almost the exact moment as the Militia's short company, under Leftenant Engels, did. The Taurians had brought a force composed mainly of tanks, supported by a lance of BattleMechs, and the Warren force was roughly equal, but with an extra 'Mech. As the largest machine in the formation, Kevin's *Marauder* was guaranteed to draw fire. He welcomed it.

"Don't let them reach the town," Engels said. "We want to do this with as little collateral damage as possible."

Taurian hovercraft sped toward Cobalt, leaving a trail of dust devils in their wake. Their lance of 'Mechs held the rear, anchored by a *JagerMech* that likely began life sporting the sword-and-sunburst insignia on its chest instead of the horns of Taurus. They advanced slowly, supporting their forward units with long-range fire. Rounds from the *JagerMech*'s light autocannon plinked off Kevin's armor, causing negligible damage, but irritating him with their sheer audacity.

"Hold steady," Engels cautioned. "Those hovertanks are our priority. Grange, you're with me. The rest of you get between the Cows and the town. Double time, people!"

Reluctantly, Kevin turned away from the Taurian 'Mechs. The fight was with them, not some worthless tankers. He fired his PPCs at extreme range. A burst of static flooded his comm, and heat boiled into the cockpit. Both shots flew high.

"Damn it!"

"Keep your head, Kev," said Dean Ipswich. "Plenty of shooting to come."

To his left, Ipswich's *Valkyrie* and the *Vindicator* that had once been Kevin's rushed to cut off the hovercraft with missile fire. One spun out of control, its air skirt shredded, but the remaining three stuck to their course. They'd reach the town in seconds. Kevin fired his autocannon at range, tearing up a good stretch of desert, but nothing more. The Taurians answered with missile fire from better gunners.

Kevin began to sweat. This wasn't as easy as it should have been.

The unpredictable fluidity of battle was stressed in every Davion combat manual, intended to prepare cadets for the reality of war versus the polished, controlled simulations found in training. It never worked. Without knowing exactly how, Kevin found himself on the main street of Cobalt, standing over a smoldering tank. He couldn't even tell if it was Militia or Taurian.

Despite Engels' orders, the fight spread into the town. Civilian cars sped for the outskirts, followed by terrified people running on foot. Neither side would seek to harm them, but their homes were forfeit in this phase of the squabble between New Avalon and Taurus.

Kevin heard Grange yelling over the comm, and a cloud of black smoke blossomed to the east. He turned to investigate, and a Taurian *Shadow Hawk* offered him some laser fire, then ducked away. A *Shadow Hawk*? There had been no *Shadow Hawk* in the Taurian line. Kevin scanned the surroundings, noting each red dot on his HUD. There were many more than twelve. Movement ahead—it was a *Huron Warrior*, a Capellan design sold to Taurus, and infantry running between the alleys.

The Cows have already taken the town. Before he could say anything, the comm lit up.

"I've got battle armor!" Ipswich yelled. Kevin saw his *Valkyrie* rocket into the air off to the south. Grange and Engels barked orders while the Militia tankers and grunts hollered for them. Kevin merely waited, looking for a target.

One found him. A blocky *Thunderbolt* stepped into the street and pointed at him in a gesture of challenge. Its laser followed a second later, scoring the *Marauder*'s arm. Kevin returned fire reflexively, but missed.

He pulled back, trying to recover his concentration. Taurians in the town! How many more lay hidden? Missiles spiraled in. Kevin refocused and fired. His PPCs discharged with a cracking boom, arcs of blue light briefly connecting the two combatants. The *T-bolt* staggered, but kept its feet.

*Thunderbolt*s had a well-earned reputation as unkillable zombies, fighting long after absorbing punishment that would destroy lesser 'Mechs. This would be the *Marauder*'s first true challenge since...when? Such questions were for later. For now, Kevin had a zombie to put down. He felt the *Marauder*'s eagerness to kill. Inside his mind, he heard it.

They stood like ancient gunslingers and traded fire in the street. Armor flew in great chunks from both 'Mechs. The *Marauder* rocked from the impact, and a shrieking static like the screams of the damned tore out of his earpiece. The 'Mech staggered, keeping its feet only through the sheer force of Kevin's will. The *Thunderbolt* was closing, trying to get under the guns of its opponent. Kevin traded fire with it, backing away a few steps, then a burst of shells came from his left and tore off the *Thunderbolt*'s damaged right arm. The Cow fell back.

Leftenant Engels' *Centurion* appeared, smoke billowing from its upraised autocannon. "Let him go," Engels said. "We've got to..." He trailed off. Kevin looked out his cockpit at the *Centurion*, wondering what had confused its pilot.

"Jesus, Langstrom!" Engels sounded like he was choking. "Your leg—there's something on—*in* your leg!"

Alarmed, Kevin checked his wireframe. The armor on the *Marauder*'s left leg was breached. And the thing in it Engels was seeing still wore a Davion MechWarrior's jumpsuit.

"Jesus D. God!" Engels swore. "Is that—"

A lanky *Snake* appeared from around a tall building and blasted the Davion machines with its LB 10-X scattergun. The micro-munitions peppered Engels' *Centurion*, one impacting the faceplate. A crazy spiderweb of cracks spread from the impact point, and a splatter of red burst across the inside.

Kevin fired back reflexively, carving gashes into the Taurian 'Mech with lasers and autocannon. It retreated, short-range missiles spiraling from its chest in defense. Kevin wasn't going to let this murderer get away so easily, even if the murder had benefited him. He kept after the *Snake*, hammering it until its side split open and it collapsed over the wreckage of a fallen Militia *Valkyrie*.

Kevin paused. That was Ipswich's *Valkyrie*. The cockpit had been crushed, punched in by a metal fist.

"No!" he yelled, outraged. Engels he could deal with, but not Dean. Dean, who was everybody's friend—and perhaps Kevin's last friend.

The tickle in his mind became a roar, and Kevin...slid into his machine. That was the best way to describe what happened. It was like sticking his face closer and closer to a holovid, until he suddenly found himself *in* the holo. He'd heard of pilots becoming one with their 'Mechs before, but had thought it all poetic nonsense it until this moment. The 'Mech's sensors became his eyes, its engine his heart, and its weapons his retribution. When he let them loose again, he wouldn't miss.

A hovercraft whizzed by, spitting ineffective machine-gun fire. Kevin's lasers casually sent it skidding into an old house, which collapsed on top of it. He felt a sting across his left side. The Taurian *Shadow Hawk* ducked back around the grocery store it was using for cover. Kevin rushed at it, smashing through the adobe building like it was cardboard. The *Shadow Hawk* staggered back, surprised by the fury of Kevin's rush, and he cored its engine with two point-blank PPC shots.

Infantry fled before him, and he cut them down with his lasers. They had no place on the modern battlefield, save as unnamed casualties. Kevin slaughtered them as they ran for their APC, then blew it to hell. Another tank spat at him in protest, and died in flames for the insult.

Jumbled voices sang in his ears, but Kevin assigned no importance to them. He exulted in his bond with the *Marauder*, this oneness he'd never shared with his old *Vindicator*. Something moved down the street past the *Shadow Hawk*'s smoldering corpse, and he instinctively triggered an autocannon burst. It was impossible to tell if he'd hit through the smoke. He rushed to cut it off, smashing through more squat, red buildings on his way.

He burst through a tall chapel, shouldering its bell tower out of his way. The bell hit the ground with a *gong*, and rolled around with a *clank*. The 'Mech he'd surprised was a *Vindicator*, but not a Taurian one. It was his old 'Mech. Who was in there now? He couldn't remember. He held his fire with a supreme effort, clearly sensing the other MechWarrior's fear.

The *Vindicator* seemed to expand from within, then its chest burst outward and it toppled over. Through flowing clouds of smoke, Kevin saw the Taurian *JagerMech* farther down the long road, its autocannons now tracking him. He sneered. In no universe could a *JagerMech* challenge a *Marauder*.

He advanced slowly and deliberately, alternating PPC fire to keep his heat tolerable. The *JagerMech* backed away, its ridiculous light autocannons belching fire that did nothing more than scar his paint. It must have expended all the ammo for its larger guns, a problem Kevin did not have. His own autocannon maintained a steady stream of slugs that tore through the *Jager*'s light armor with gusto.

Then one of his PPCs blew through the *JagerMech*'s knee. The leg sagged, thigh collapsing onto shin, and it fell onto its side. An explosion briefly lifted the 'Mech up, then it rolled onto its back and lay still. Kevin advanced until he stood over it, and planted one clawed foot firmly and disdainfully in its cockpit.

Suddenly, there was nothing left to kill. The red IFF tags on his tactical display were fleeing into the badlands in a cloud of dust. Panting and sheened in sweat, Kevin felt his strange bond with the *Marauder* slip away, and he was just a MechWarrior in the cockpit again. The wireframe damage readout told him he'd lost armor across the entire 'Mech, but only taken internal damage to the left leg. He tested the movement, found it was fine, better than ever. The special lubricant had worked.

Cobalt smoldered around him. Unchallenged, the *Marauder* dominated an avenue of wreckage. No tanks waited to insult his dignity, no BattleMechs remained to question his authority. But that wasn't quite true. There was one more 'Mech, still alive. His HUD just didn't identify it as an enemy.

With the halting gait of a sleepwalker, an *Enforcer* emerged from behind one of the few intact structures. It took a few steps into the street, then seemed to sense the *Marauder* staring at it through the wisps of smoke and froze, the gazelle caught in the gaze of the lion.

There was only one *Enforcer* on the field today. "What have you done?" Grange's voice ached with horror.

Kevin glared at the 'Mech, still panting, but oddly emotionless. "I've destroyed the enemy," he said. "Isn't that what we're supposed to do?"

"You've destroyed the town! These are *our* people, the ones we're supposed to protect. You trashed their homes, their school, their church."

"Collateral damage. It happens."

"Not like this." Tears ran in Grange's words.

"I *saved this world!*" Kevin shouted. "*Me!* I've defeated the Taurians. Isn't that worth a few buildings, more or less?"

"You call this saved?" Another cloud of gray smoke obscured the *Enforcer.* "You haven't defeated anything. This was one company. The Cows came with over two regiments! Didn't you hear the leftenant? Before you went on your little rampage, we'd received orders to pull back. Not just to base, to the starport. The Taurians have won—we're leaving. Ingram's already off-planet, the rest of us aren't to be far behind."

"Ingram's a worthless coward," Kevin spat. "You leave. Go on, follow the great general. I'll stay here. I'll stay, and I'll solve the Taurian problem, alone if I have to." He ground his clawed foot into the cockpit of the fallen *JagerMech.* "I'll carve them up and send the pieces back to Taurus in a matchbox."

"Listen to you." Something besides horror had crept into Grange's voice. It was close to fear, but worse. It was the feeling a person gets when he realizes just how badly he's screwed up. "It's gotten to you, son."

"For crap's sake, Sarge, don't start that again!" Kevin was livid. The fool was going to blame the 'Mech again. Always Grange and his haunted 'Mech, the cause of all suffering in the universe. Kevin was sick and goddamned tired of it.

"I'll start it if I think that's the problem! Look at you. Look what you've become. Would the man who came off that DropShip five years ago have trashed a whole town over a few lousy Cows? Would this have happened before you got in that—that *thing*?"

Kevin said nothing, glaring at the battered *Enforcer*. It stood in the same slightly hunched posture Grange assumed when chewing out one of his grunts, twitching in the same subtle ways.

"You're going to have to give it up."

"*What?!!*"

"Give it up." Grange enunciated each word clearly. "Get out of it before anything worse happens."

Give up his *Marauder*? This 'Mech was his life, more important than food or drink or the warmth of a woman. Now that he knew what it could do in combat, what he could do in it, he would *never* give it up, especially not so Grange could dump it down another dark hole to rot. He wouldn't let the old man do that to him again. The itching beneath his scalp grew maddening.

"Forget it."

"Son, I ain't asking you." Grange's voice fell into his ears full of sadness and threat. "Get out of it right now. You're coming back to base with me, and that's going to be the end of it. We're pulling off this world, and that thing's staying behind. Let the Taurians have it. Our last revenge."

Outrage twisted in Kevin's chest at the thought of his 'Mech in the hands of a filthy Taurian cow. He would never allow it. *Never.*

Grange had spent most of his life in a 'Mech cockpit, and could read another MechWarrior as easily as a children's book. When Kevin's shot came, his battered *Enforcer* was already moving, and only a single laser grazed its left arm.

"Don't do this, Kevin!" Grange yelled. The *Enforcer* jumped backward, taking refuge behind a flaming building.

Effortlessly, Kevin slipped back into oneness with his *Marauder*. His PPCs demolished the *Enforcer*'s scant cover. Heat flowed over him in murderous waves. Out of the smoke came a laser beam, scoring his 'Mech's arm, but failing to penetrate.

"I'll have you, old fool," someone growled.

Grange was through talking. If fighting was his only option, then he'd take the offensive. The *Enforcer* rocketed over the rubble, its autocannon roaring. This time the shells tore through the skin on the *Marauder*'s torso. That screeching static filled Kevin's ears, and he screamed.

The *Marauder* outclassed Grange's *Enforcer* in every way. It had taken more damage, and the *Enforcer*'s pilot was more experienced, but the old man still stood no chance. Too many years of frustration rotting in a stagnant purgatory had found their outlet. With the resolve of generations of Federated Suns soldiers, Grange stood and delivered. Lasers and autocannon shells were traded, charged particles arced, armor melted and ran. In the end, as in life, hate overpowered reason.

With both arms blown off, the *Enforcer* pointlessly fired the anti-infantry laser in its torso until the *Marauder*'s PPCs vaporized the last of its armor and shattered the shielding over its engine. Its heart gave with a terrific blast that leveled the rest of the buildings all around. Riding the upward wave, rockets flaring, the *Enforcer*'s ejection seat carried its charge away from death, setting down somewhere within the smoldering ruins of Cobalt.

With his last enemy vanquished, Kevin returned to his cockpit with a howl of triumph. He laughed, loud and free. Despite the crippling heat and the blood from wounds he hadn't realized he'd received, he felt better than he had in months. The weight that had been growing on him had lifted at last. He reveled in the sensation, letting the *Marauder* cool. As his mind returned to reason, the concept of consequences began to intrude on his peace, but they were vague and could wait until—

His HUD buzzed. It had painted a half-dozen new targets in red, sitting in his rear arc. He'd been so distracted tearing

Grange's 'Mech apart that he had completely failed to notice their approach, and now they were well within optimum range. He spun to face them, realizing as he did that something was different. These were not Taurian machines, and they certainly weren't Militia.

His comm crackled. "Nice show." The voice crawled out of his earpiece slippery and slimy, like the voice of an eel. Kevin hated the speaker instantly. "And to think all we came here for was the bank. I should thank you and the Cows for the distraction. In and out with no problems."

Suddenly, Kevin knew who this was. He'd been hearing about them all month, this band of pirates who'd taken a liking to Warren's financial institutes. Through sheer luck, the Militia and the Taurians had clashed in the very town they had chosen as their next target. But was it luck? Was it really?

There were six 'Mechs, all lighter models, none a real threat to his *Marauder*. Even damaged, he could take them if he needed to. Cautiously, they fanned out before him, their leader speaking from a dingy *Phoenix Hawk* dummied up with a horned helmet. Chained across the torso were three humanoid forms, though whether they were real bodies or only mannequins Kevin couldn't tell.

"I'm curious," the pirate said, a smile in his slithery voice. "Why would a Federat blast another Federat? Other than the obvious joy such an act brings, I mean. It just doesn't seem like the behavior one expects from two comrades in arms."

Kevin eyed the pirates warily, but not with apprehension. Their half-dozen ragged machines stood tense, skittish before him. Only the leader held his 'Mech with a confident swagger, displaying his extreme arrogance.

The *Phoenix Hawk* waved its hand at Grange's shattered *Enforcer*. "What'd he do? Sleep with your sister?" The pirate's henchmen chuckled like good little sycophants.

"He wanted to take my 'Mech," Kevin said.

"Say no more. Where we come from, a man's 'Mech is his worth. Try to take that from him and you get...well, you get what he got." The eel's tone switched to casual nonchalance. "So whatcha gonna do now, Feddie? Did you have any plans for your buddy beyond blasting him out of his 'Mech? Because

I think he's still running around out there." Out in the debris that used to be a town before Kevin found it.

Yes, Grange would still be out there. The old man was too mean to be injured in his ejection. He was there watching, and he knew what Kevin had done. No, he knew what the *Marauder* had done. Grange would blame the 'Mech, and now he'd make it his life's mission to destroy it. The only question was what he'd do to Kevin.

"The way I see it, you got two choices." The *Phoenix Hawk* strutted, the chained bodies on its chest swinging merrily. "You'll be facing court-martial for this. If I remember my Feddie justice, it's execution for attacking a fellow soldier. Of course, you could go find him and squish him, but I'm sure there are *other* witnesses."

Kevin thought the pirate was implying that he and his men would testify, but movement in the ruins caught his eye. People were crawling out of the rubble, digging frantically or calling out for loved ones. One dust-covered man stood dazedly in the cratered road, apparently oblivious to everything, including the bloody stump where he'd once had a left arm. These people saw the ring of 'Mechs within their wreckage, and they knew which was responsible. Fingers were already pointing.

"So, two options," the pirate said. "Number one, stay here, get court-martialed, lose the very 'Mech you just fought oh so hard to save."

Kevin's gut clenched. The whispering in the back of his brain had not departed when Grange's *Enforcer* fell, and it growled loudly at the pirate's snide tone. No one would take his 'Mech. His hands closed on the conn. Six of them, one of him. But he was a *Marauder*.

"Or door number two." The slimy smile was back in the eel's voice. He began to walk around the *Marauder* as he spoke, gesturing to the heavens. "You could leave this worthless dustball behind. Leave the whole Federated Suns behind! Come with us, live the life of a pirate, and know what it is to be truly free. Pillage, plunder, and kill whoever you want, it's all fair game!"

The pirate's voice quickened. "Join us, Grady's Grinders! Late of Malagrotta, bound for better fortunes. Accept me as your captain, have the courage to follow where I lead, and I'll show you freedom and the wonders of a life unhindered by the chains of law and order. We're bound for Tortuga, where I've got a friend who wants to rebuild the Fusiliers. I'll bet we'd be most welcome, especially if you and, ah, *your* 'Mech came along. What do you say? Want to be a Fusilier?"

Kevin blinked. Hadn't he been trying to become a Fusilier recently? It seemed so long ago. Yes, he had wanted to be a commander in the Fusiliers. What difference did it make *which* Fusiliers?

The choice loomed over him. Salvaging his situation would be difficult. He could possibly pass the civilian witnesses off as shell shocked and mistaken, but Grange was still out there, hiding, watching. Kevin would have to hunt the old man down, then he'd have to destroy the *Marauder*'s battleROM, a procedure he felt unequal to, having never located one in the cockpit.

And then what would he have to look forward to? A return to a unit he despised, that despised him? A retreat off this world ahead of the Taurian juggernaut, until the next one where he'd just have to fight them again? Staying here and living in hiding under the Cows' occupation? None of that appealed to him. None of it fit. The back of his mind assured him of that. He and the *Marauder* were destined for better things. Grady the Eel was right. This world couldn't offer them anything, perhaps the entire Federated Suns couldn't.

"I accept," Kevin said. It made sense. He was a marauder, it was his nature. "Tortuga it'll be. But just so you know—"

He raised the *Marauder*'s right arm, and with casual grace triggered the PPC. The blast took the *Phoenix Hawk* square in the face, coring the cockpit and venting excess energy through the back. The silly prosthetic helmet tumbled down, knocking loose one of the chained bodies. The headless 'Mech remained standing for a moment, its posture reflecting confused shock, before toppling over with a crash.

The other pirates raised their weapons, but none fired.

"*I* lead," Kevin said, sweeping an arm across them. "*You* follow."

Contented static crackled in his earpiece. Tension stretched across the seconds, then the 'Mech on the far right of the pirate line, a worn *Stinger* that had probably seen service in the Reunification War, lowered its laser and straightened.

"DropShip's just over that ridge." The MechWarrior indicated a distant rise. "Captain."

Captain. Kevin liked the sound of that. It was a start.

Hoisting the dead *Phoenix Hawk*, the pirate 'Mechs fell into formation around their new chief, and together they set off for their ship, and the call of Tortuga.

The call of the stars.

CENTURION
MEDIUM—50 TONS

ENFORCER
MEDIUM—50 TONS

JAGERMECH
HEAVY—65 TONS

PHOENIX HAWK
MEDIUM—45 TONS

PLOG19

SHADOW HAWK
MEDIUM—55 TONS

THUNDERBOLT
HEAVY—65 TONS

VALKYRIE
LIGHT—30 TONS

PLOG19

VINDICATOR
MEDIUM—45 TONS

RAVAGER

RAIDER'S ROOST
TORTUGA PRIME
TORTUGA DOMINIONS
8 MARCH 3080

Listen to me and I'll tell it true. I'll tell you this tale of Charlie Blood, a shining example of purest Tortugan scum. Born in squalor, raised a slave, fought his way outta the pens by twelve and into the barracks by fourteen. He was gonna be a MechWarrior, Charlie was. He'd march across the stars, taking what he wanted and laying waste to the rest, and any Filtvelter or Davionista or Colonial Marshal in his way could take a dirt nap, courtesy of Charles Bloodworth III.

Charlie was here on Tortuga Prime when *he* came—the man with the dead eyes, the one they called Black Kevin. Yeah, real original we pirates are, but "black" *fit* Kevin Langstrom. Black heart, black soul, black 'Mech. Some said he was the devil; some said he was the devil's own son and Lucifer had disowned him. Those in the know, when you got enough drink in them, said Black Kevin wasn't the devil. He was just a tool, a pair of idle hands the Dark One had put to use. Those broken minds, no matter how sozzled, were consistent. Kevin wasn't the source of all evil. It was his 'Mech. The *Marauder*. The "Dark One."

Charlie Blood heard these tales, relishing the shivers down his spine as each miserable sot spilled them past drink-rotted teeth. Horror, gore, rapine, all the wanton ills Charlie dreamed of, and atop the pile sat Black Kevin and the Dark One. Gold, women, more gold, more women—all the things someone valued if they called themself a pirate. One day there'd be a new king atop the heap, and his name would be Charlie Blood.

There Charlie was, sneaking into the 'Mech bay under full moons, a pilgrimage with three other cully wannabes in tow. Steaks for the dogs, a bit of coin for the guards—gold, that is, since the C-bill took a shit—and into the bay they went. Oohs and aahs for the machine gods, the bringers of death Charlie and his buddies would one day pilot to glory. Spit and rust compared to what sat in the Great Houses' hangars, but here they made kings of men. Row after row, *Brigand*s, *Javelin*s, *JagerMech*s, and even a few chassis leftover from the Word's final days stood shoulder to shoulder. The pride of Tortuga.

And one 'Mech all alone, back in a corner no lamp ever brightened. Eternally in shadow, was the Dark One. Even brightest sunlight shunned it.

Someone broke out the booze, and on the foot of an ancient *Warhammer* they made their vows. Glory, plunder, vice—such were Tortugan dreams. The second bottle was stronger than the first, the third even more so, and then they made their dares. Who would climb to the top of Harpoon Annie's *Centurion* and piss on her cockpit glass? They laughed as Obed did the deed, giving that nasty bitch a good coating. Who'd peg a guard hound with this empty bottle? Fernando barely made it back through the door and still lost a bit of his pants, earning many raucous laughs.

Who would touch the *Marauder*? Just walk up and touch it?

Silence.

Soulless men feared across the whole of the Dominions dared not lay hands on the Dark One—who the hell were they? Four young cullies full of booze, not courage.

"I heard he sleeps in the cockpit," panted Fernando.

"Well, he's not there now," said Marcus. "He was in the MechWarriors' Hall when we left, with Sally Strapless on his knee."

"I still ain't doing it. He'll know, cully. He'll know right when you touch it and be out here like smoke. Then it'll be *you* sealed up in one of those legs!"

"He don't do that!" Charlie scoffed. "It's rumor, stories to keep smegheads like you in line."

"You think so, Bloody Chuck?" Obed said. "Then *you* do it. Go on. Show us what you got!"

So of course Charlie had to show them. He was Charlie Blood, not some crier from the pens. He swigged the last of bottle four, tossed it to smash in the dark. "Bunch of gullible smegs."

They walked with him to the head of the last row and peeked around the gantry. *It* was still there, lurking in the corner, a smoke jaguar poised to pounce. Someone shoved Charlie forward, and even his shriveled little heart skipped a beat.

"Go on, Chucky," Obed taunted.

So up went Charlie's chin, and a-shrivelin' went his nuts. Damn—he wished he had some water, his mouth was so dry. Was that his heart, trying to kick its way out? Two bays away, and looking back all he saw were three heads peeking around the gantry.

Stupid smegheads. His vision blurred in slo-mo ripples. A few dry blinks to clear it, another staggering step, and he was in the cubicle, almost near enough to touch.

So cold, so dark.

Charlie looked up.

The *Marauder*'s head turned to face him.

That's ridiculous, he thought. *It don't have a separate head. It can't do that.*

But it had. The *Marauder*'s long snout pointed impossibly toward him. Its torso had bent just forward of the arm joints, the way a shark might turn its head. He could even see the scrunched-up sections of armor inside the bend that were the gills of that shark. It had turned, all right. It was *looking* at him.

Then the 'Mech opened its mouth, and Charlie ran. Until his death by a Filtvelt firing squad four years later, Charles Bloodworth III swore to anyone who would listen he'd seen rows of serrated teeth in the Dark One's maw.

But what kept him out of the 'Mech bay from that point on and ensured he never emerged from the bottle again, he said, were them eyes.

All five of them.

"Horse hockey," Fat Tony said. "Hell's horse hockey."

"Hey," I said, "I'm just tellin' it like I heard it." I tapped out my cig and flicked the butt at him. "You asked. You said, 'Tell us a story, Eddie.' And I did. Truth ain't my job. You want truth, go squeeze it outta Charlie's corpse."

"Charlie Blood had a sponge for a brain, and he kept it soaked in gin. I wouldn'a trusted him to find his way down if I tripped him."

"Bad habits come from someplace." I waved my pack of cigs at him. God, I wanted another, and damn me if I didn't take it. "When do you think Charlie dug into the booze? Right around the time Black Kevin showed up, that's when."

Tony just grunted. He didn't believe, but it didn't matter. He still listened, and he'd listen the next time.

"S'true! I seen it! I seen it!" said Twitch, that tic under his eye going. "You—you go down there late at night sometime. It *looks* at you, see? It knows you're there, and it don't like you snoopin' around. No, c'mon, I'm telling it true!"

The other dozen or so cullies in my audience were rolling eyes, with advice like "Stuff it, Twitch" and "Look at this spazz-head."

"Sure, sure," Twitch said, "laugh at old Twitchie. Kick him and laugh, but who knows *him*, cullies, eh? Who knows Black Kevin? Who's been with him every job since the first, eh? *Eh*?!" He threw wild eyes at them, but no one looked back. Not that they were afraid, just that Twitch wasn't worth it. "That's right, cullies. *Twitch*, that's who. S'me and only me knows him and what's true 'bout the Dark One. Only Twitchie! Ha! Haha! Gimmie a hit off that bottle, Eddie. C'mon."

"Keep it," I said as I tossed him my brew. God knows I didn't want it back after his lips had been on it.

Booze was Tortuga's national vice, worshipped on a world where what water you could find tasted like day-old piss. Twitch was into the bottle something heavy, along with other recreational distractions. Cigs, Spazz, K-Z, even the exotic stuff that floated over from Canopus. If it took you out of this world, Twitch vacuumed it up. Idiot even swigged coolant.

He wasn't this bad when he'd arrived, clutching the coattails of Black Kevin. He was the last of Grady's Grinders, one of those nobody gangs that usually ends up dangling on the short end of a long rope. The Grinders hadn't run afoul of no Marshal, though; they'd done far worse. They met Black Kevin, but Grady alone had paid the piper that day. The rest chose to follow the Dark One to Tortuga. One by one they'd died too, until just Twitch and his useless old *Stinger* carried the Grinders' legacy.

He'd been a normal man then—scuzzier than most, but normal. Six years beside Black Kevin took a toll on a man, and whatever parts of Twitch's abused body that weren't already dead just festered, waiting to be lopped off. He'd done it to himself, but if you believed the legends, the Dark One was draining his soul.

My story was over, and now they were all going at it. This was my favorite part, sitting back and watching these scholars of the pirate world debate. Fat Tony yelling, Oscar yelling louder, Twitch being totally ignored as he bounced between thoughts trying to interject his own nonsense. I didn't have to say anything, I just had to smile and shrug whenever anyone asked me to clarify. I just tell it like I hear it...with maybe a few embellishments.

Then the hush fell. Anyone working this hub knew what that meant. *He* was here. You didn't have to see him to know. You could tell because your mouth was suddenly dry, your palms sticky, and your cullies turned space-sick green.

"Gentlemen." So soft, that voice, like velvet. When he spoke, you damn well listened. And we did, a dozen fools with uncomfortably full bladders. "Ravannion's posting a new contract for bidding tonight. I rather like the rumors I'm hearing. I need five good MechWarriors, but I'll settle for you lot. Who's in?"

"What's—" Fat Tony's voice broke like a schoolboy asking out his crush. He cleared his throat, found some macho. "What's the take?"

"Five percent, plus extras."

He was generous, Black Kevin. Made working for him tolerable, sort of. Extras meant whatever plunder you picked up for yourself: kick over a jewelry store along the way, and you keep whatever you can carry away. Twitch's greedy eyes flashed as he raised his hand.

"Knew you'd be up for it, Twitchie. Always in for a little fun, aren't you?"

That growl in his voice wasn't praise. Twitch simpered like a beaten dog, which is exactly what he was, I suppose.

"Well, who else?"

Fat Tony was in. Five percent was a lot toward his idiotic plans for retirement. Oscar, Otego...

"And you, Eddie. You know I want you."

Damn it. He always wanted me, for my stories. On long runs you spent six, eight months in space, something had to keep the cullies entertained. My gift, my curse. What the hell could I say?

"I'm in."

"Good. That's settled then. Bidding opens at twenty-two hundred."

Then he was gone, smoke in the wind. We sighed, pulses returning to normal. Otego crossed himself, mumbled something to Jesus. Might seem like a contradiction, a pirate praising God. Casual observers thought we went the other way or were at least atheists, but one can't be born into Tortuga's lowest depths, raised to prey on your fellow man, taught killing and thieving were your only means, and *not* believe. We all believed in God; we could just never figure out why He hated us so much.

After all, He'd given us Black Kevin, and the Dark One.

This was Tortuga. Never mighty like the Houses, never as ambitious or filled with grand designs, but just cunning enough to not draw the full attention of those behemoths it fed on. Hey, we existed the only way we knew how. Our worlds were barely habitable, requiring outside help to remain viable, and since the fall of the Star League we'd had little help. The Great Houses occupied themselves laying waste to their own worlds, so ours could rot away all by their lonesome. No one cared until the Word of Blake showed up.

Things were all right under the Word. We got high-speed rail connecting the seven major cities, and better water purification meant fewer saps dying of dysentery. Shitting yourself to death is no way to go, I say. All we had to do in return was step up raids and hit Word-designated targets. Not a bad trade. Yeah, things were looking up for Tortuga, but then the Robes just up and left. Something about an attack on Holy Terra, how dare the infidels, defend the Master, Blake be praised, blah, blah, blah. They bailed, and we've been spiraling like a flushed toilet ever since. Tortuga was reverting to its nature, but for the briefest moment we'd had a taste of civilization. Only a taste, but maybe it would be enough.

At 2200, we gathered in the war room, the vaunted Tortugan Roost. The Blakists built this compound, and when they moved out, the lords moved in. In the Word's day we had a precentor, but today we have a king. Ravannion was our king, and no more cunning and underhanded a soul existed on Tortuga Prime. Rumor held he'd murdered all his competitors in a single day, consolidating his power behind a row of spiked heads. Ravannion claimed to be descended from some famous Kurita officer, but who the hell cared? Couldn't prove it one way or the other. We had idiots claiming to be descended from Alexander the Great, Melissa Davion, and even Mother Jocasta. On Tortuga, your own blood didn't matter. What mattered was whose blood you could spill to get where you wanted to be. Ravannion had spilled plenty.

One by one the lords filtered in, entourages in tow. Mikhail the Kinslaughterer, wearing his Manei Domini-esque prosthetic arm. That pretty boy Darrian Worlish, toting another devilish beauty on his arm. Gonna have to get her name, for sure. Timore, the supposed former Ghost Bear, thrown out of his Clan for being a Crusader among Wardens, whatever that meant. Fifteen of the foulest scum the Dominions could cough up spread out along the tiered seats, looking down into the center where a large holotank sat, their miens ranging from eager to apathetic.

Jobs surfaced through Ravannion's web of informants, and here the lords gathered to bid on the take. Pretty simple concept, really. Whoever promised him the biggest cut got the job. There was more to it of course—subtle political currents ran through the whole process—but that's the basic gist. Ravannion gave the details, sometimes recommended a force, then let them go at it. He retained the right to reject any bid, and occasionally he ignored protocol and assigned a mission like he was some kind of real commander and not just the shiniest turd. Then he sat back and awaited their return with his loot.

No work and all the reward. It's good to be the king.

Ravannion appeared by the holotank, wearing that damn purple-silk sash.

"Friends! Brigands! Men—and women—of good taste! Welcome, one and all!" He always opened bidding like this. Idiot fancied himself some kind of entertainer. "Tortuga's finest, gathered here tonight to spread the glory of her name—"

"Get to it!" shouted a fool whose blood alcohol level exceeded his IQ.

"No appreciation for ceremony? I swear, you lot get more degenerate every day. Reminds me of something my dear old mother used to say—"

"Afore or after the raxx reamed 'er?"

BANG! Ravannion drew his sidearm and shot the cully. This might seem barbaric, but remember where we are. It elicited laughter, not horror. Even I sniggered, until I caught Kevin out of the corner of my eye, his arms crossed, a glower strong enough to melt steel.

Ravannion waved his smoking gun as the assembled scum cheered. "Anyone else? I do requests."

"Just get on with it," Kevin muttered, but for our ears only.

"And tonight's target is..." Ravannion thumbed the holo switch, and a blue bubble popped into view, sprinkled with continents and red-dot cities. "Defiance! Perhaps you curs have heard of it?"

A couple of nods, a couple of shrugs.

Kevin's lip curled. "Point Barrow Combat Region, Minette Operational Area, Crucis March. Federated Suns."

"Right in one." Ravannion flashed his crocodile smile. Never affection in those chompers, especially for Kevin. "And what makes this world special, you ask? Come on, anyone? Anyone? You cullies need to brush up on your history. How's this: do the words Task Force Serpent ring any bells?"

A couple intrigued nods at that, and Timore spat.

"Yes, thought that might get a reaction, even in this bastion of ignorance. Serpent bit the Clans in the behind when they least expected it, but what does that have to do with Defiance? Anyone? Ah, never mind. Before setting out for the Clan Homeworlds, Task Force Serpent mustered on Defiance. It was the base they launched from."

Kevin shifted. Those dead eyes were alight now, and hungry.

"It's not the Serpents we're interested in, boys and girls, it's what they left behind. Ten regiments of 'Mechs. They were bound to have left a few in the gantries. Several, from what I hear, and I have it from a source that's never told me wrong. The Serpents were on a deadline, and anything that wasn't ready at launch time got left behind, stashed in a warehouse for later. Only later never came. Lots to think about when they got home, like siblings taking their petty rivalry galactic. At some point, the guards said, 'Screw it,' and that warehouse was just locked up and forgotten. Even when the universe was having that little disagreement with our former Word benefactors, no one bothered to investigate one dusty warehouse squatting in a no-name town on a backwater world."

Everyone was muttering now. Mikhail stroked his chin with that Manei-claw, and Darrian Worlish's escort was practically melting into his ear.

"And there it sits to this day. A company or two of BattleMechs for the taking. They may be a bit beat up, but I'll wager our friends at Vengeance can get 'em running. So, bidders, begin!"

Timore opened with 10 percent, which was laughed at.

"Clanners are supposed to take bidding seriously, Timore! Your disguise is slipping. Try harder."

Timore turned red, and there'd probably have been a Trial of Grievance if Timore didn't know Ravannion would just shoot him. Leland the White went with a slightly less ridiculous 12 percent, Mikhail fifteen.

Kevin held back. Arms crossed, a smirk that was almost a sneer curling his lip, he just watched as his competitors drove Ravannion's cut up and up. The war broke down to just Worlish and Mikhail—24, 25, 27 percent.

"Thirty-two and a half percent," Kevin said.

All eyes rotated his way.

"I was wondering when you'd speak up," Ravannion said. "Can't do a Suns raid without Black Kevin at the fore."

Mikhail shook his head and sat back down. He gave Kevin a rude gesture that didn't come across quite right with that mechanical arm.

Worlish's pretty teeth gnashed. "Thirty-four."

"No," said Ravannion, still looking at Kevin as he stroked his beard. "No, I think I'll invoke king's privilege here. I think Mr. Langstrom knows something you perhaps don't, Darrian. The FedSuns are his old stomping grounds, after all. Very well. Sold to Black Kevin for thirty-two and a half percent!"

Worlish's friend unlaced her arm from his and twisted into a feminine knot, beautiful face gone real sour. Darrian was sleeping in a cold bed tonight. Good. I felt better about getting her name.

"That's a huge cut," Fat Tony muttered in my ear as Kevin went down to blood the deal. "Almost nothin' left for him, after he pays off the dropper and jumper cap'ns. What's he playin' at?"

"He knows something." It was Twitch, in a surprisingly lucid moment. "Ravannion's right. Kevin's playing two games here, maybe more. And so's the king. Look at him."

Behind the hand stroking his beard, Ravannion smiled like a shark. His eyes never left Black Kevin.

MERCHANT-CLASS JUMPSHIP *BARRATRY*
NADIR JUMP POINT
TORTUGA SYSTEM
18 MARCH 3080

"Defiance? Pretty deep in."

Krokus wore an eye patch. Can you believe that? In an age of cybernetics, that asshole wore an eye patch. Stylized himself some kind of old Terran pirate, that one, and all he did was drive the damn ship. Proud to have not been groundside for sixty years, which meant our pirate captain hadn't so much as taken candy from a baby since the Third War.

"I know where it is," Kevin said. "I'm telling you to cut our travel time as short as you can. I want to arrive at least a week before using standard routes says we should."

Krokus sighed. "Who're we racing?"

"It's the Suns. I don't want to spend any more time there than necessary. We get in fast, we get out fast."

Kevin's hate for the Fedrats was legendary. His past was a fog of rumor, but Twitch said he'd been a Feddie officer once, until he killed his whole general staff and made off with the 'Mech, that horrible *Marauder*-like thing ensconced in Bay One of our nameless *Union*. There was a Kevin Langstrom on some Suns most-wanted lists, but for piracy, not desertion. Still there was that hate, especially for someone he called the "Old Man." Kevin was meaner on Suns worlds, edgier, as if waiting for a shoe to drop. We needed to be fast because the Old Man was out there somewhere, the Old Man was coming. Wasn't fear, not exactly, but more caution than he showed on Calderon or Fronc worlds, for example. Hushed speculation about the Old Man ran in smoky barracks late at night. No answers ever surfaced, not even from Twitch, but one thing was for sure: whatever unnerved Black Kevin was to be avoided at all costs.

"I can do it," Krokus replied. "But it means hot-charging the core. That's not recommended in the best of times, and this ain't exactly a new ship."

"It'll work," Kevin said.

The funny thing was, nobody doubted him. He said it, thus it was so. Never mind that the *Barratry* was about 5,000 years old, with more holes in its jump core than a kilometer-long block of Swiss cheese. Kevin said it would work, so it would. He knew piracy well, but somehow he knew jumping better.

The trip sucked, like space travel always does. It's so damn boring, and on ships with busted grav decks you get all kinds of sick if you don't take care of yourself. You've got to exercise every day or your muscles will atrophy, and running laps in zero-g just ain't an option. Lots of resistance weights, or lots of old-fashioned zero-g wrestling with sweaty pirates, all betting on who'll go unconscious first. Yeah, I'll take the weights.

And who was the entertainment? Yup, good old Eddie and his stories. Thirty, sometimes forty cullies gathered in the lounge, all hushed and wide eyed as I spun my tales. I never thought I was that good, but I guess the intelligence of your audience has a lot to do with how easy they are to keep enthralled. Most of this lot would find Timore's Clan tales too sophisticated. When they couldn't corner me for a yarn I spent my time alone, drifting down by the core or staring out a porthole into the black. Nebula-gazing can be relaxing to the frazzled mind. Jumps came a lot more frequently than I was used to, which also sucked. Being shoved through another dimension always left me queasy, with a bad pulse behind my right eye.

One jump out from Defiance, I was alone in my favorite star-gazing spot, dreaming about Darrian Worlish's hanger-on named Saccharine. Saccharine, so sweet. The bulkhead door opened, and my stomach flipped. I swallowed into my scratchy throat. *Oh, damn...*

"Eddie."

Right in my ear. "Jesus-damn-God-mother—Why the hell do you—"

"Relax, Eddie," Kevin said. "I'm not going to kill you, or... otherwise."

Comforting, but I'd have believed it easier if he'd added "yet."

"I like you, Eddie. You show a man the respect he's due. Even Twitch. You'd be a good man in another life, a respectable man. That's why I'm going to share something with you. When we're dirtside, I want a second pair of eyes I can trust."

"If it's all the same, Cap'n, I'd prefer—"

"Shut up."

I don't need to be told twice. I drifted away from the porthole so I could look at the man instead of his ghostly reflection. Damn those dead eyes.

"Listen close, Ed. I don't care about beaten-down 'Mechs or money or anything else. I wanted this job because Task Force Serpent had maps—maps that led to the Clan Homeworlds. But if you think they didn't carry every bit of knowledge about what's beyond the Periphery, then you're dumber than the average pirate. I want those maps, Eddie, and if there's even the slightest chance something lingers in this Serpent cache, I'll take it. While we're down, you're going to keep your eyes and ears open for anything resembling a star chart, understand?"

"Aye, Cap'n."

The bells began to sound for jump; the *Barratry* was headed to Defiance.

Kevin pointed through me, at the bulkhead. "That way, that's the heart of the Suns, the Davions, and beyond them the rest of the Sphere. But what's over here, Eddie? What star is that? Do you know?"

I had no idea which dot he was pointing at. It didn't matter anyway, he didn't want an answer. I just shook my head.

"So much is out there, waiting. The Star League explored far beyond its own borders. They found things out in the deep, things no one should ever have found, then brought them back. Sometimes that wasn't a good idea. Maybe some things didn't want to be taken so far the light of home no longer reaches them. But just because there's no light doesn't mean you can't be seen."

Two bells.

"We're small creatures, Ed. Tiny little things, protozoa in the ocean of the universe. Do you know what protozoa are, Eddie? Of course, not. Raised out in the nowhere, you're lucky you can read, aren't you? They're insignificant, protozoa. Just like people. The difference is those protozoa know their place. They don't strive to be more than the meaningless little parasites they are. People don't know when to quit. They meddle, Eddie, they meddle, and poke around in places they don't belong."

I admit it, by this time I was sweating. Being alone with him was like being caged with a lion. And here he was talking about humanity like he was no longer a part of it, like he had somehow cast off his nature. I could feel my lunch trying to escape, much like I wanted to do.

"Humanity has broken some laws it never should have touched. Eyes are on you, and do you know what they see? Do you *want* to know?"

I shook my head. God damn, I did *not* want to know, couldn't he see that? *You betcha*, he wanted me to answer, I could see it in that crooked smile. But he never did say. He did worse than that. He showed me.

The final bell sounded, and the *Barratry* jumped.

I can't describe it. We don't have the words. We are, as he said, too small. I'll try, though. For your sake, and for my own catharsis, I'll try. I remember an impression of scale, of size, like zooming out and out and out until everything—the ship, the sun, the galaxy—dwindled into a speck, a dot in a petri dish. And there I was, and there *they* were, the ones whose laws we had broken. They knew we were here, and worse, they knew I was among them. Something bigger than my mind, bigger than the combined capacity of all human imagination, tasted my life with a barbed tongue. God, the pain.

I thought I was screaming, felt like my lungs would rip apart from it. Fear, that was the easy part. What set me off was the helplessness, the futility, not just of my own life but of all humanity. Kevin was right. We were tiny, insignificant, and we did not know our place. For all our striving, all our great arts and sciences, all that humankind had accomplished throughout these transitory millennia, we were nothing but uppity bugs. And the boot was coming to stomp us out.

Like waking from a long dream, I found myself bumping gently against the bulkhead, legs curled into my chest. I was sweating bad, and lunch had escaped.

"I've heard of a world." Black Kevin's voice, calm over my sobs. "A place where the Star League poked through, and the beyond bleeds into our universe. The night side glows, like perdition. Destiny, Eddie, and...destination. That's where their footsteps lead. Or begin. Defiance—even Tortuga—is just a stepping-stone. Clean yourself up. We launch in twenty."

DEFIANCE
CRUCIS MARCH
FEDERATED SUNS
29 MAY 3080

Defiance was like any other Outback dump, if a tiny bit more developed. We came in at a pirate point less than a day out, and Krokus started hot-charging the core again. Kevin wanted to be in and out ASAP; the Old Man was on his mind.

We hit the dirt unmolested, putting down a good distance from Ravannion's coordinates. Kevin's doctrine called for misdirection; we'd raid a few towns far away from the Serpent warehouse to draw off local support, then double back and hit it hard, bringing in the dropper to haul off our loot.

Three APCs of fools and a fourth to carry off the, er, *cargo*, zipped ahead of our 'Mechs. These were manned by our PBI conscripts. They'd get nothing of the take except what they carried off themselves. Most of them just came along for the fun, their rewards being food and maybe a chance for a hot shower. Kevin gave them an hour in the first town, under the guns of our 'Mechs. Watching these guys work was like a ballet of chaos. Nothing of value was left unplundered, nothing of beauty unmolested. Their sacks of booty bulged, and the fourth APC filled to capacity as this little burg burned.

Fat Tony pinged me over a private comm. "Ed. Anything seem, I dunno, *off* 'bout this job?"

"I don't follow."

"Supposed to be a couple companies of 'Mechs in this cache, right?"

"So Ravannion says."

"So, a *Union* only carries twelve 'Mechs, and we're already six. Kevin planning to stow the rest as cargo, or does he mean to leave us all here?"

I saw where he was coming from, loud and clear. That giant percentage Kevin had promised Ravannion wouldn't hurt so much if he didn't have to pay out our five each. Still, according to his own word, he didn't care about this job. No haul meant no pay and no need to cut expenses.

"I'm all for 'wait and see,' Tony," I told him.

A pause. "I just want to know you got my back if things go south."

"Always do." I swallowed. Crossing someone like Mikhail wouldn't hurt much, but turning on the Dark One? I think my shivers ran down my 'Mech's spine.

The next town was two days later, and this time the MechWarriors got to take our turn, all except Kevin and Fat Tony. Tony said he was satisfied with his 5 percent and didn't need any extras, but I knew he was keeping an eye on Kevin. Not that his *Shadow Hawk* would stand a chance against the Dark One, but it was a nice gesture.

We went down in pairs, first Oscar and Otego, then Twitch and me. Sloppy seconds is bad, trashy thirds even worse. Both banks were flaming ruins, and the only jewelry store looked like a tornado had crapped in it. I swept up a pile of mostly broken glass with a gem or two mixed in while the fools shot it out with local law enforcement. The liquor store was trashed, but I found a stash of cigs in a corner market. My brand, too. Some days I love being a pirate.

I was rushing back to my *Brigand* when I saw it: a library, with three terrified faces pressed against the windows. I had ten more minutes. Why the hell not?

"You know," I shouted as they ran screaming into the back. "A bolt lock isn't worth jack if your door is made of glass!"

I tossed a few books into my sack. If I was lucky, there'd be a new story for me to spin for the cullies. The place was piddly, but ComStar had networked it into the planet's database. Worth a look.

Jackpot. Took less than a minute to download what I needed, then back into the street I went.

Heavy weapons fire. Aw, crap. I raced up my 'Mech's chain ladder, slammed on my neurohelmet, and had her moving before I was even properly strapped in. A hovercraft wearing the sword-and-sunburst insignia zipped by and peppered me with SRMs.

"—fast strike force!" Fat Tony radioed. "VTOLs and hovertanks, maybe some PBI on hoverbikes." A boom over the comm. "One less VTOL. Call it, Cap'n!"

"Oscar, Twitch! Cover the fools. Tony, Otego, cut us a path out. Northbound, cullies! Ed, start a fire."

My *Brigand* was an -X3 model, equipped with PPCs and flamers. The blazes the fools had set were cheery campfires compared to mine. Less than a minute later, the smoke billowing from this town could hide a DropShip.

I headed north, catching up to Otego's *Quickdraw* as he covered our exit. The Feddies didn't follow. I watched a pair of VTOLs circle the town as the fire-rescue people went to work. Good that they knew their priorities, good for us.

We ran for almost an hour, until the smoke was gone from the horizon. Fat Tony pinged Kevin for a plan.

"We'll keep this course another few clicks, then turn for the cache. Send all but one of the APCs back to the dropper—"

Suddenly, Twitch's *Stinger* turned and darted into the trees.

"Twitch!" Fat Tony's *Shadow Hawk* shook a fist. "Twitchie! Get your ass back here!"

"Let him go," Kevin said. "That nose is smelling something besides cocaine."

Twitch disappeared into the brush, the rest of us tailing after. We found him by following a column of smoke. Twitch was climbing down his chain ladder to inspect the ruin of a tank he'd apparently just killed all by his lonesome. My battle computer IDed it as a Hi-Scout. My eyebrows went up. Sophisticated stuff.

Kevin thought so, too. "Ed, go down and back him up."

I popped my hatch and clambered down, Sternsnacht in hand. Twitch rooted around in the tank's hold, entering through a hole he'd kicked with his *Stinger*. The crew weren't going to be a problem, so I holstered my gun. Twitch had already stripped them of any useful goods and was now rifling through the tank's stores.

"How did you know this was here, Twitchie?"

"Saw sumthin' movin' in the bush. Thought it was an animal at first, but it kept comin' back. Watchin' us, followin' us. Finally got a good look and scanned it. HUD pinged it as one o' them PathTracks, so's I knew he were hidin' out here somewhere. Tried to lead me away, but I didn't fall for it. Sniffed 'em out, I did! Can't hide from ol' Twitchie!"

Say what you would about the man, but he was a damn good scout.

"That PathTrack ain't gonna be a problem later on, is it?"

"No, no!" Twitch shouted. "I seen one of these on Malagrotta once, in Tiqualme's gang. Look here!" He pointed into the tank's rear.

I got a good look at the most complex control panel ever, all manner of monitors, joysticks, switches, and controls I couldn't even name.

"That's where he sat," Twitch said. "That's where the bastard was snoopin' from. Betcha he been followin' us fer days. Just sittin' back here, like playin' a vidya game! It ain't fair, man, it ain't!"

He drew his laser pistol and put a spiteful hole in one monitor. "Ain't no worries no more, Eddie!"

Static on my comm. "Time's up, cullies," Kevin ordered. "Leave that thing for the fools. We're making for the cache."

It took us four more days of cross-country running to reach the cache. Ravannion's info led us to an abandoned barracks a click or two outside a big town. Kevin sent a couple fools on foot to scout. They came back after a few hours spying from the bushes to report no activity.

"We waitin' 'til dark, Cap'n?" Tony asked.

That'd be the logical thing to do, but—

"No. No, we move in now. Otego, signal the dropper. Tell them to set down as close as possible. Smash-and-grab protocol, boys. After I knock down that door, the fools will go in to designate priority targets. Then you cullies get dragging."

Pirates love 'Mechs with hands. We'd pair up to haul off whatever machines we found in there, Tony and Otego grabbing the heavier stuff, me and Oscar the light, while Kevin and Twitch stood guard. The PBI could load any spare parts. I'd done a dozen similar raids without a hitch.

"Dropper ETA two hours," Otego said.

"Move," Kevin said.

The Dark One outgunned the rest of us together. One volley would disintegrate even a reinforced door. But it didn't need to. When he stepped into the open, that warehouse door began to roll up. There were 'Mechs inside, all right, just not the ones we were expecting. Nope, these marched out in formation, just a lance's worth, but accompanied by twice that many tanks and a crapload of infantry.

The lead machine was an *Enforcer III*. It opened a general comm. "I hoped it would be you. Ravannion didn't make any promises, but he knew what I wanted."

"We been crossed!" Tony hissed. "We runnin' or what, Cap'n?"

We were all dancing on a wire, waiting on Kevin's orders. I could almost see waves of rage emanating from the *Marauder*. It stood like an animal with hackles raised, facing down a company and more of hostiles with no indication of backing off.

"There is no Serpent cache?" Kevin hissed.

"Never was," the *Enforcer* pilot replied. "Just a ruse, and it worked."

"He betrayed us. He betrayed *me*." It was Kevin's voice but...it wasn't. It was deeper, fuzzier, like a transmission from far, far away.

"He wanted to get rid of you. You're poison, boy. Bad luck." The guy sounded earnest, honest, like a beloved old uncle. "Everywhere you go will be the same. No one wants you around. No one wants *it* around."

My secondary monitor flashed. Orders were popping up, tight-beamed just to me. I relayed them to the others.

"I swore I wouldn't do this," the *Enforcer* pilot went on. "Told myself to shoot on sight, that there was no going back for you. But I can't. All this, it's my fault, not yours. So I'll ask you one last time. Give it up Kevin. Come quietly, son, and I'll do what I can to protect you."

"We've been through this," Kevin said. "Back is a direction I don't go."

"There's no other option, son. I ain't joshing you. Shut down or I'll put you down."

Kevin had an answer ready, an alpha strike for the biggest Davion 'Mech. That was our cue, and we all cut loose. I torched everything in range, and Fat Tony's rotary autocannon was going so hard I thought he was standing on the trigger. The Davions scattered, all except that *Enforcer*. With parley over, it came in guns blazing. I had a feeling I knew who this was, and yup, I wanted no part of him.

Everything was burning, belching thick gray clouds into the Defiance sky. It was now or never, and Oscar and Twitch knew that, too. I was hightailing it with a *Stinger* on one side and a *Javelin* on the other.

"Get back here, you cowards!" Kevin growled.

A PPC beam sailed by, close enough to flick static across my monitors. I skidded to a stop, and so did Twitch. The *Javelin* kept going. Kevin yelled at Oscar to get his ass back here, and I prayed he'd listen. Nope. A shadow fell over my *Brigand*. The Dark One rippled with malice. Oscar was almost a kilometer gone, kicking up dust. Not far enough. That PPC crackled again, and the *Javelin* fell. Headless, I would later see. Pirate loyalty, pirate justice.

Kevin turned on us. "The smoke is darkness, and all darkness is mine! Get in there and roast them. Kill everything that moves."

If death were looming, I'd rather let the Davionistas do it. At least they couldn't touch my soul. Into the fire I went.

Twice the smoke parted enough for me to see Twitch shredding Davion PBI with his machine guns. Once I saw the *Marauder*, though... To this day that is the one memory I most wish I could erase. It was like I could see it better in the smoke, see it *truer*. It was a grotesque thing at the best of times, but here in the darkness and death it came through clearer than ever. I felt like a fish looking at a lure and thinking, *yeah, that's another fish, like me*, then suddenly perceiving the line, the rod, the entity at the other end, and its intent.

God be with me.

We might've had the fury, but the Davions had the numbers. Eventually we fell back to the city, stomping through its streets like madmen. There's always a bit of fun in that. Watching cars spin away, people scatter in screaming masses—it makes you want to chase them. I guess what they say about running from predators is true.

Deadlock set in. The Fedrats wouldn't come guns blazing into their own city, especially knowing we had no qualms about burning it all down, but we couldn't get out either. Kevin holed us up in an airship hangar, hidden from flybys. Nobody else was down, but we all showed damage. My armor schematic was a bloody web of missing panels, and Twitch's 'Mech had lost an arm.

Amazingly, the fools had stuck by instead of hightailing it. Probably saw what happened to Oscar. Kevin sent them out with orders to fill that APC to bursting then stood guard while the rest of us raided the hangar's stores. I found some hoagies abandoned by fleeing civvies, and shared with Fat Tony. One for me, two for him.

"This is horse hockey, Ed," Tony muttered around a mouthful. "Ravannion sets Kevin up, and we get to be collateral damage?"

I nodded. "It happens. Look at it this way: at least you don't have to cross Kevin."

He shuddered. "Yeah, but now we gotta rely on him to get us outta here. I tell ya, retirement sounds better after every job."

"This might be retirement, big man."

"Not for me, cullies." Otego dropped down next to us. "Thirty-five 'til the dropper lands, then we're out of here. Take what we got and run, I say."

"Five percent of nuthin' is still nuthin'," Tony muttered.

"S'what you get for not grabbing any extras!" Twitch said, sour-faced.

The fools returned, chased by a wave of police who broke and ran when the *Marauder* poked its malformed head out of the hangar like a dragon defending its hoard. The APC was loaded with civilians, as many as the fools could grab, which was a lot. Men, women, children in sobbing rows, all aware that God had abandoned them. Otego took guard as Kevin came down to inspect the haul.

"Funny time to be picking up cargo, Cap'n," one of the fools said as Kevin went down the line.

"These aren't cargo." Kevin's grin made even that cully squirm.

This hangar was loaded with chain and wire for the airships, and on Kevin's instruction we put it to use. Every one of the poor sots was chained together and chained across the front of our 'Mechs. Some of the fools got a good kick out of hauling our meat shields into place, but I saw one or two go off into the corner to puke. At least there were a few humans left among us. My *Brigand* wore a necklace of sobbing metros, and damn me if I didn't feel a pang of sympathy for 'em. Tony, Twitch, and Otego got similar, but the Dark One was our captain, and captains get their due.

Two women covered the barrels of the *Marauder*'s PPCs, and the woman on the right was very, very pregnant. They screamed and screamed, but I don't think it was from fear. They lay against the Dark One's hot exterior with nearly bare flesh. Any sane creature would scream until there was no sanity left to shout away. The sound made my skin crawl, and Fat Tony was a gray blob trying to hold in his beans. We were pirates, and that meant a bit of murder on a rough day, but at the end of that day we were still human. Kevin, he had...transcended. The Dark One had brought him across whatever rift I'd seen when the *Barratry* jumped, and what it brought back had no humanity left. He did what he did not with the glee of the insane, but the derision of one squashing a trespassing ant.

Those girls weren't all. Attached to each leg by a long tow-chain came a gang of victims. They'd need to run fast or be dragged, and if Kevin kicked the 'Mech up to full, that was the end. And of course, he'd put some older people in the line.

Fat Tony stepped up to Kevin like a man walking a minefield. "Is—is all this necessary, Cap'n?"

"Intimidation is a weapon greater than any gun." He slapped Tony on the shoulder, and I thought the big man's heart might burst. "Innovation is what sets a good pirate apart from a great one, Tony. Might cannot win our day, but theatrics will."

Our dropper hit dirt just outside the city. The opposite side, naturally, which left us to run through a couple clicks of city blocks. Kevin had us moving in moments. We didn't encounter resistance for a few blocks, but then we turned a corner and there they were. The Davions arrayed themselves in a wall between us and the grounded dropper. The *Enforcer* was in the lead. Their advance stopped when they got a good look at our decorations.

"Are you insane?" hissed a voice over the comm.

"What do you think?" Kevin answered.

No reply, but the *Enforcer* trembled with outrage.

"I do what I need to," Kevin said. "I look out for me, like I should have done from the beginning. God knows I can't trust anyone else to do it."

"I looked out for you. I always did. But damn me, I fouled it all up! Damn me..." This was the voice of a man who would be weeping if he had any tears left in him.

"Your trap has failed, old friend. Not even you can label this as acceptable losses. Get out of my way."

"It owns you. There's nothing left now. I'm sorry. I'm so sorry."

I don't know who started shooting first. That part is blessedly gone from my memory. In fact, most of that battle is a haze lost in my own tears. I remember lashing out with my one functional PPC, reserving my flamers for the sake of the poor sots straddling their barrels. I kept looking toward that sphere on the horizon, wondering how I'd been running toward it for hours, but it never got any closer.

Night fell, and we were still running. Tony and I got separated from the others doing a cat and mouse with some hovercraft in a warehouse district. I sent one Regulator to its maker, then a Gauss slug from the other caught his *Shadow Hawk* in the cockpit, and that was the end of Fat Tony. Too bad, I always liked the guy—but not enough that I hadn't done some poking to find out where he kept his retirement stash. He wouldn't be needing it now. It's amazing what little minutiae flit through your mind in the middle of battle.

It seemed this night would never end, not until Davion's endless minions brought justice to me. I had visions of being impaled on that damn sword, incinerated by that sunburst, having my heart ripped out and eaten by the resurrected Fox himself. To this day I hate raiding Suns' worlds, and Defiance is why.

Somehow, Providence delivered. Heavy long-range-missile fire swatted the tank tailing me, and I looked up to see that rusty *Union* towering over me. It was so beautiful! I ran up the ramp, skidding into the bay and sending a dozen cullies scurrying. Twitch followed in his now armless *Stinger*.

There, we waited. Five minutes. Ten. I didn't dare pop my hatch yet, in case whatever came out of the dark required my guns.

A shapeless blob coalesced from the smoke. It didn't wear a sword and sunburst. It wasn't so much a machine as a wounded animal, skinned, and bleeding coolant down one leg. Rent shards were all that remained of its dorsal autocannon, and it walked with a pronounced limp. The chains dragging from its legs were empty, mostly. The Dark One thumped up the ramp without pursuers, master of all.

"Otego?" I asked.

"Dead." Kevin's voice sounded wearier than I'd ever heard it. "Prepare for liftoff."

"Is it over?" Twitch whispered.

"Nothing is ever over, Twitchie."

That was it, then. No point in waiting any longer. I parked in a bay and dropped out, noticing on the way down that my 'Mech had lost its necklace. I was shaking like Twitch on a binge. All I wanted was a shower, a cig, and a ton of booze. I'd be locking myself in my cabin for the entire journey home, and if any cully tried to hit me up for this story, I'd space their ass.

"Oy, Cap'n!" shouted a deck hand. "Your wench, she's still breathin'. What should I do with her?"

Somehow, Kevin had never fired his right PPC. The girl he'd chained across it, the one with the big belly, God had decided to punish her. She was conscious and intact except for some torn skin where the chains had dug in. Her bottom lip trembled, but she was finished screaming.

Kevin squinted at her like a curiosity. "Cut her down, let her go. Maybe we should come back in a few years, see what comes out, eh?"

I had no words, just a nod. Anything to get his attention off me, to get that damned smile to turn away.

The girl staggered toward the bay door, arms tucked into her chest, a length of chain trailing from one foot. No one touched her. She looked back at the verge, unsure of her freedom. I don't think anyone expects pirates to look at them with pity. Then I made a mistake: I looked her in the eye. I got cold. Now, there was another.

Kevin spent most of the return trip in the hold, repairing the Dark One. None of us except Twitch were allowed in there while he was working. Not that we complained. We didn't want to crawl in that thing's innards, end up like old Twitchie. Together they got the *Marauder* patched up, except for the missing autocannon. The remains of its housing stayed bent, like a jagged dorsal fin. Oddly, Kevin didn't have the rest of us prepping for a fight. We'd all been betrayed, and the PBI wanted some blood to show for it when we got home. Me, I didn't take things so personally. Ravannion wanted Black Kevin out of his hair, we were just collateral damage. Too bad for us. Thus were the politics of Tortuga.

It was a few weeks before I remembered the datastick I'd downloaded from that library. With any other lord I'd have leveraged it for more gain, but not with Kevin, and not in the mood he'd held since we left Defiance. I just found him in the galley one day and gave it to him, with an apology for forgetting about it for so long. He plugged it in, and I swear to God he actually smiled, slow and all contented like in the glow of that star chart. A thousand light-years of spinward Periphery, courtesy of the Explorer Corps and Task Force Serpent, recently declassified and available only on Defiance.

"Good work, Eddie. Good work." He poked a spot in the map. "And there it is. Destiny and destination."

"So, are we changing course?"

"Oh, no." Those eyes, they weren't dead now. "I have one final bit of business to wrap up on Tortuga. Our dear king needs his cut."

"No offense, Cap'n, but is it wise to go back there?"

"Trust me." He grinned, and damn me if he hadn't sharpened his teeth. "They'll talk about this for generations."

Our dropper touched Tortugan soil almost exactly six months after we had left. Life hadn't changed here, but it was about to. Oh, yes.

We expected Kevin to rampage through the city, smashing everything in his way. No mercy for Ravannion, none for his cronies. But that's not what Kevin did. I think, when I saw him walking out of that ship, a little bit of my faith in God died.

Kevin walked on foot, but not alone. Behind him, like a protective parent, strode the Dark One, its cockpit popped open to show there was no one driving. No more pretending. The devil had come back to hell, and justice was in the air.

It was damn unnerving to see that *thing* walking down the street all on its own, but somehow not surprising. We'd all suspected who really called the shots in that unholy pair; this was just confirmation of our fears. Our gang of fools trailed them, shouting and firing into the air. The scum of Raider's Roost lined the streets as Kevin's parade marched on Ravannion's stronghold, many cheering, some just falling to their knees. I lagged behind, trying to blend in. I kept looking for Twitch, but he was nowhere to be found. In fact, I hadn't seen him since before we touched down. Probably hiding in a bottle somewhere, waiting to see which monster was going to come out on top today. Wise strategy.

As Kevin and the unmanned *Marauder* approached the Roost, a wave of humanity clogging the streets behind, Ravannion's crowd came out to greet him. Ravannion himself was on foot. What a jackass. He thought he had to meet Kevin as an equal instead of at the controls of his *Black Knight,* that doing so would somehow make his victory more legitimate. His guards weren't that stupid. They ringed the area in active 'Mechs, but not a one fired. Even when Ravannion shouted at them to vaporize Black Kevin and his master, not a one of them moved. The writing was on the wall, the crown in flux.

I was so deep in the crowd I couldn't hear properly, but I recognized when Kevin gave his formal challenge. Every pirate had the right, but few ever exercised it. Kevin chose to fight unarmed, or I assume that's what he meant when he unstrapped his sidearm and tossed it away. Ravannion couldn't just shoot him now that a formal challenge was in effect. No one would respect him if he broke the only law Tortuga had. That, and the Dark One was standing right there, PPCs leveled. Even from this distance I saw the whites around Ravannion's eyes, the knowledge that his reign ended today.

It was decided so fast the front row barely had time to gasp. Kevin grabbed the king about his neck and choked the life out of him with his own sash, until his face was as purple as that silk. Then he hung Ravannion's corpse above the door to the Roost, upside down, so that anyone going in could reach up and yank his hair like a bell cord. The king was dead, long live the king!

And that was it, really. As usual, the news reports blew it all out of proportion, always focusing on the Dark One. Zoomed-in shots from above showed the whole cockpit, empty as factory new. No one was hiding in there, it was walking all on its own. Talking heads shouted out miracles and damnation in equal measure. One side was closer to right than the other, but the population gobbled it all up. They had a new king, and the devil wasn't so bad when he was on your side.

I stayed in my quarters for a week, drowning in booze and smoking my way through the cigs I'd bagged on Defiance. Cullies kept coming to my door begging for the tale. I told the first dozen to get it from Twitch, but he still hadn't turned up. Found himself a nice little hidey-hole, did Twitchie, and was probably doped into the next century. The knocks kept coming, and eventually I just ran a live wire to my door handle, taking what pleasure I could from the surprised shouts.

Then one day there came a knock, quiet and respectful, and my stomach clenched.

"Hello, Eddie," that velvet voice said as I opened the door.

"Cap'n." I swallowed. "Or do you prefer I call you king now?"

"Doesn't matter. I suppose for my legacy's sake you should say king, though there will be a new king soon." He came in, helped himself to a bottle of my booze. "Tortuga holds nothing for me anymore. This was a stepping-stone on my journey, and I've lingered too long. There's work that needs doing, out there in the deep. It commands me go, and go I will."

My heart shriveled into a prune. "You want me to go with you, don't you?"

He stared at me for a long time, every second of which I thought I might melt.

"No. You stay here, Eddie. You stay and tell my tale like only you can. Let all these lowlife failures and those who come after know Black Kevin is still out there, watching. Don't let them disappoint me."

Then he was gone, like smoke. A DropShip departed within the hour, and I never saw Kevin or that black *Marauder* again. Though my heart has been lighter for it, I still wake up in the occasional cold sweat. Always on the anniversary of that last jump into Defiance, I wake up weeping and remember there just might still be a boot coming. You tell yourself it's impossible, all trickery and bad hallucinations, but is it? You never know 100 percent what's real and what's beyond real. There's always a niggling little doubt, like the atheist who still thanks God for little miracles. That's why I have my booze so close these days, because even in the most rational part of my mind, I'm still not sure.

I do know that months after Kevin and the Dark One vanished into the black, we found Twitch. Some techs traced a bad smell to a disused storage room in our *Union*'s hold. The door had been welded shut. Twitch was in there, with some empty booze bottles and an odd piece of leftover machinery. Most of the resulting stories focused on Twitch's condition, how his fingernails had been torn off as he'd tried to pry his way out, how his belly was full of glass from trying to eat the bottles. No one talked about the bit of machinery, they just thought it was something Kevin used to lure him in there before sealing it up tight. I never did get a chance to examine it, but I got a look at the holo one of the techs took when they opened the compartment. Looked a lot like the rig in the back of that Davion Hi-Scout.

I don't know more, and I ain't sayin'. Truth? You figure it out. That part ain't my job.

I just tell it like I hear it.

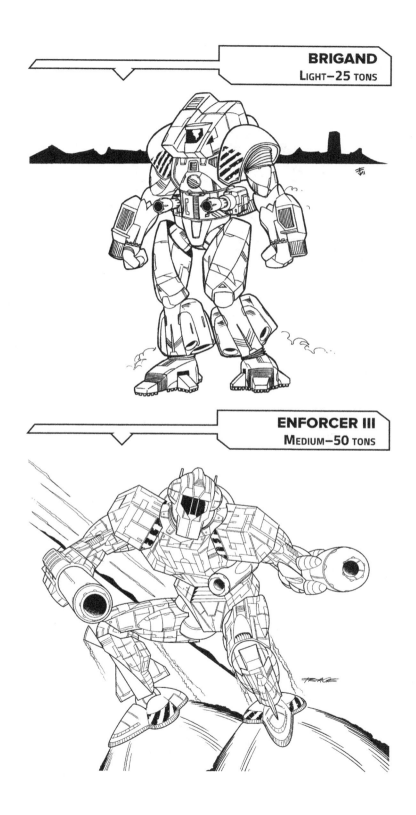

BRIGAND
LIGHT—25 TONS

ENFORCER III
MEDIUM—50 TONS

JAVELIN
LIGHT—30 TONS

QUICKDRAW
HEAVY—60 TONS

STINGER
Light—20 tons

GHOST HUNTING

Universal law dictated that bars the galaxy over be dark, smelly places populated by alcoholics sucking on their bottles like ticks about to pop and the assorted lowlifes who fed on them. In these havens of vice and sin, boots stuck to the floor, fistfights were immediately bet on, and those with enough coin could find more prurient entertainments with just a glance. A vast array of 2D screens projected everything from sporting events to local politics to the latest *Immortal Warrior* entry, all at maximum volume. Here aboard Zenith Station, miners of the Mica system rubbed shoulders with *yakuza* enforcers, low-end Davion nobility on a poverty vacation, and at one table along the wall, Brother Perseus Schell, Knight-Errant of Randis, and his cohorts.

Pritchard leaned over to shout in Percy's ear. "Just to be clear, I hate Micanos. I hate Mica Two, I hate Mica Seven, and I hate Zenith Station. Very specially hate Zenith Station." He cast an appraising gaze over the assorted drunks, prostitutes, and thieves. "And I hate you, Percy. Just thought you should know."

"Noted." Percy sipped his tea and glanced around. Their food was late, and the waitress was ignoring them. That's what happened when you ordered tea in a land of liquor, but Percy wanted the three of them to stay sharp. He scanned the patrons again, hoping to see one specific face. If he'd just show, then Percy could be on his way, and Pritchard might stop complaining. No, that would only happen after the stars burned out and dust collapsed back unto dust, but if that one face appeared, then at least there would be movement. The man, his information, Percy's information...and maybe more. Maybe war. And maybe even against the right enemy.

Idania's eyes flitted over three men laughing nearby, and she flinched when one of them leaned too close. Nerves. Percy almost told her to show a bit more décor, but remembered he'd never had to evaluate every male as a potential threat.

She leaned in, wringing her hands. "At least we won't be overheard in here."

Pritchard held a hand to his ear. "What?"

"At least we—"

"WHAT?"

"Knock it off." Percy never needed to shout to be heard. He checked the time, local and standard. "We'll give him another hour, then head back to the ship. Try again tomorrow."

"What if he never got the message?" Idania asked. It was a valid question. Hyperpulse-generator communication was a thing of the past, leaving interstellar messages at the mercy of JumpShip captains who may or may not be going your way. Spotty at best, but it was all they had out in the Periphery.

"Or if he says no?" Pritchard added.

Percy shook his head. "Our mission doesn't change if we're short one person. I've heard a few rumblings, and I believe our interests might align."

"You're putting a lot of faith in chance, Percy."

"Faith sustains me."

A man appeared at their table. Tall, blond, and unmistakably drunk, he laughed as his hip collided with the back of Pritchard's chair. "Your pardon, my short and ugly friend. How careless of me, I've spilled your drink. Here, have some of mine." He poured some green concoction from his bottle into Pritchard's tea.

"I don't want—get out of here, you—" Pritchard half rose to shove the interloper away, but Percy yanked him back down.

"Lucien." Percy gestured to a chair, and the newcomer melted into it. "We were just talking about you."

Pritchard looked about to choke. "You mean this—this is—"

The stranger half bowed. "Star Commander Lucien Clearwater, Snow Raven Watch."

Idania pulled down her glasses to get a better look. "The Red Raven? You?"

"You were expecting something else? Something plumed and savage, perhaps?"

"You just don't seem like a typical Clanner," Pritchard said.

"Met many?"

"Well, I—"

"Oh, stuff it, Pritchard." Idania held out her hand, which Lucien Clearwater pretended not to notice as he sipped his drink.

Percy smiled somberly. "Best to let go of your expectations. Lucien revels in shattering them."

A tangle of at least three bodies rolled past their table, harried by a formidable woman screaming and delivering kicks into the pile. Lucien Clearwater raised his bottle to them. "Why am I here, Brother Perseus? Other than by choice, obviously."

"We're bound for Novo Franklin. One of our brothers disappeared there while investigating supposed pirate activity."

"Normally I would say that sounds like your problem, but there is that word, 'supposed.' It has a tendency to...shatter expectations."

"Knights of Randis don't go down easily, at least not to pirates. Two brothers went to Novo Franklin to investigate a *hostis humani* situation. Only one came back, but he left his 'Mech behind, along with his mind."

"And I take it you want me to help you find one or the other?" Clearwater contemplated something under his fingernail. "Doesn't sound like an effective use of my time. Why don't you send your ugly little friend here to scare information out of the Franks. Lord knows he frightens *me*."

Pritchard snarled, but Percy restrained him with a hand. "You said the same thing about New Port Royal, Lucien. Remember how that turned out? Most fun you'd had in years? And I did save your life."

"And I refit your 'Mech. We're even."

"Maybe I'm in the market for another refit."

"Then ask the Sea Foxes." Clearwater sighed, and something resembling seriousness came over him. "My nation's border is getting very noisy, and you want me to go ghost hunting on a farm? I am sorry, Brother Perseus, but I cannot justify it. I wish you well."

He rose to leave, and Percy tossed a data disc onto the table. Lucien eyed it. "My birthday is in October, Percy."

"Then consider it a bribe. Or blackmail, if you prefer."

The Red Raven sank slowly back into his seat. He produced a datapad and inserted the disc. All traces of humor and the fuzziness of drink disappeared. He stared at Percy with unblinking eyes, and Percy stared back. "How do you know this? And why does Randis care?"

"Word travels in the Periphery, HPGs or not. The Brotherhood knows you lost a Star of 'Mechs out there in the dark. The Council doesn't know where or why, but I have some ideas. Would you care to confirm them?"

"A Star was lost." Lucien Clearwater leaned back in his chair, his gaze calculating. "Where and why are not your business, but I assume you know how?"

"Destroyed by a single 'Mech. A 'Mech with unnatural accuracy, that moved less like a machine and more like a living being. Five casualties in as many minutes. The last one never recovered because—"

"Because his cockpit was locked from the inside." Idania shivered. "But he wasn't in it. I've heard that story, too."

Percy folded his hands and looked expectantly at Lucien, who was chewing his tongue as if it had gone bitter.

Pritchard rubbed the bridge of his nose, as he often did when the conversation turned in a direction his faith couldn't follow. "Ghost stories again. You do understand Percy's proclivity toward things that go bump in the night, don't you, Mr. Clearwater?"

Something cold blew over the table. "*Mister* Clearwater?"

Pritchard turned a shade of green. Lucien Clearwater suddenly seemed much more like a typical Clan warrior. "Err, I meant no disrespect, um...sir."

"'Star Commander' will do." Lucien shook his head and turned back to Percy. "Cutting through your bullshit, as a typical Clanner would do, you want me to come with you to Novo Franklin because you think the culprit may be found there."

"I want your skills with me in case he is. I want your *White Raven* at my side, and the best MechWarrior I've ever known piloting it." Percy gestured around the table. "Three wheels don't make a car. Four do. What say you?"

Lucien smiled, a ray of sudden joy that lit up the grunge. "Colorful metaphors will get you everywhere, Brother Perseus." He grabbed a bottle off a passing waiter's tray and accepted a slap on the back of the head for it. "A toast to seal our pact." The four of them clinked glass, but Lucien held down Pritchard's hand. "Not you, I poured coolant in that drink."

He downed his bottle and slammed it on the table. "Bargained well and done. I will pick up some assets and meet you on Novo Franklin. You remember our frequency?"

"I remember." Percy nodded, and Lucien Clearwater melted into the crowd as suddenly as he had appeared.

Pritchard eyed the contents of his cup. "Quixotic soul, isn't he? You don't think he caved a bit too easily?"

Idania shook her head. "He made up his mind as soon as he read that disc. The rest was just for show."

"How do you know him, Percy? The Red Raven is a legend. You're just..." Pritchard waved a hand as if to say *Well, look at you!*

"We worked together a while back, cleaning out a nasty problem on New Port Royal, Tortugan space. It's where I picked up this." He placed on the table a dagger, jagged and ugly, with a splintered wooden handle and a blade black as ink.

Idania picked up the irregular knife and turned it about, trying to catch a sparkle of light, but it remained as black as the void outside the viewport. "It's 'Mech armor, isn't it?"

"A shard from the 'Mech of Black Kevin Langstrom. The skin of the Dark One itself."

Idania quickly placed the knife back onto the table. Pritchard crossed himself and muttered a ward.

Percy smiled. "No curse has ever manifested in the time I've had it. But then I do keep it in a dybbuk box, just in case."

"Pray that it's working," Pritchard said.

"Must be. Or maybe this isn't from the Dark One at all, and the pirate I took it from lied to me with his last breath."

"Oh, I think it very much is." Idania had that look about her, the one trait Percy wanted most on this mission. "When you told me...I could feel it. Feel the truth of it. What have you gotten us into, Percy?"

"Just a little ghost hunt."

NOVO FRANKLIN
THE PERIPHERY
1 JULY 3151

Novo Franklin could have been a garden utopia. A stable, fertile world with a mild climate and no native threats, it should have become a powerhouse of food production for the entire Spinward Periphery, but the colonists fleeing the Reunification War brought little of civilization and all of mankind's ills. There were farms, to be sure, but instead of being harvested by high-tech, automated combines the size of a house, most were worked by a single weathered farmer and a team of oxen, and god forbid their plow break and they have to haul it fifty kilometers by horse cart to the nearest blacksmith. Such was life on Novo Franklin.

Some lucky fiefs did retain the technology of their ancestors, and their lands prospered most. With those profits, they chose to kill each other in ritualized BattleMech jousts and other displays of stupidity. A freelance mercenary with a 'Mech could live high on Novo Franklin, growing fat on celebrity. And since no warrior on the planet had the skill or ruthlessness to stop them, many a pirate also prospered here.

"Aye, we got 'em," the first consul to greet Percy's company nodded. "Can't go a moon wit'out some dirty bunch o' mudfoots droppin' in somewhere. Steal what they can, burn a few fields, slaughter who they like, and not always the cattle. Mudfoots don't care. When your soul's gone, what's there t' care about? Runnin' 'round in the mud, not even a shoe. Mudfoots, ya see?"

Percy couldn't hear through the man's accent, but Pritchard seemed to grasp it. "Are they always on foot, or do they have 'Mechs?"

"Aye, sometimes. Big ol' hands to be grabbing big ol' handfuls o' plunder. Sometimes one o' our boys drives 'em off, but if'n one thing's a'sure, a bastard's got brothers. They'll be back, an' this time with a real anger in 'em. Usually best t' just let 'em take what they will and leave."

"If you make it easy for them, then they'll just keep coming back," Idania said. "Maybe we can make it a bit harder, and give you people some of the Lord's peace."

The old man chuckled in the way the elderly do, but he gave them a lead. "Parson landhold. Two hunnert or so kilometers nor'-nor'east. Burnt t' ash, so I hear. If'n you do find any mudfoots, give 'em the what-for from me!"

"As long as there aren't too many of them," Pritchard muttered as they parted. "We're not loaded for bear here." Knights-Candidate were not usually allowed BattleMechs, but Percy had a way of convincing people, and the Grand Knight had allowed him two machines the Brotherhood could afford to lose—a *Fire Javelin* for Pritchard, and a *Chameleon* for Idania, both old Davion salvage, with Crucis March Militia colors still showing through their paint.

Percy slapped Pritchard's back. "The flag of Randis makes a nice force multiplier, at least against 'mudfoots.' It will do until Lucien gets here." Until then, they were three MechWarriors and a few technician Squires in a banged-up *Buccaneer* DropShip, alone in an unfamiliar land.

"I still think you could've gotten me a *HawkWolf*," Pritchard moaned.

"Why? It's a stupid 'Mech with a stupid name. Do you know how many 'Mechs have 'hawk' or 'wolf' in their name? It's a lot."

"I'm just tired of driving junk. When I was apprenticed to Lady Huntington, I had to clean her *HawkWolf*. It was so new I could smell the leather."

"Newness isn't important. Effectiveness is, and the *HawkWolf* doesn't have it. We operate out here sometimes for months without resupply. Old Brother Toccera addressed our needs with a 'Mech wholly reliant on ammo, and not a lot of it. When Lucien refitted my *Archer*, the first thing I asked for was more ammo and more lasers."

"Do you think it will be enough to stop the Dark One?" Idania asked softly. "Do you think all of us together will be?"

"With Lucien as our ace? Maybe."

"And does the Dark One believe that?"

"God has set us on a path, and we will go where he leads. If he sends us into hell, then we'll march through with our heads held high."

Two days later, the comm lit up with a cacophony of raven calls. Percy sent back a set of coordinates, and within a few hours the rumble of massive feet shook the old warehouse they had rented as a headquarters. A gigantic bird of a BattleMech, bright red and accompanied by two Anat APCs, parked itself beside Percy's *Archer.* Lucien Clearwater descended its chain ladder as the APCs disgorged several dozen graying, weather-beaten warriors.

Lucien hiked his thumb at a man the size of a small bulldozer. "Star Commander Sid. Leader of this rabble by dint of being the biggest and most capable of stringing together a complete sentence. Freeborn and *solahma* one and all, hungry for battle and ready to die for the cause. Now, what have you got for us to hunt?"

NOVO FRANKLIN
THE PERIPHERY
5 JULY 3151

They traveled cross-country for two days, until a faint beacon detoured them to a lazy river meandering through a prairie in which herds of Franklin bison roamed. These were wild beasts, introduced by colonists but long since escaped from bondage. Flat-bottomed clouds fat with rain skated across the sky, with spears of sunlight poking through them like the fingers of God.

In one of these sunbeams stood Pritchard's *Fire Javelin,* pointing to the river. "What do you make of that?"

A series of rocks poked through the water, creating minor rapids. Only they weren't rocks, but a unified mass that glowed on Percy's magnetic-resonance monitor. In this land walked by no one, someone had left something behind.

The company gathered round, in water knee-deep to their 'Mechs, to witness a fallen comrade. The elements had scoured away most of the 'Mech's paint, but enough blue remained to be a match for Percy's own colors. "A *Valkyrie.* This was the 'Mech of Brother Thaddeus MacEoghan. Help me, Pritchard."

They grabbed the *Valkyrie* under its arms and dragged it ashore, the 'Mech dripping mud and river grasses like a drowned cadaver. Sid scampered onto its back and picked at the hatch in its head. "Sealed. I will need a cutting torch."

"Can you tell if anyone's inside?"

"Ferroglass is too murky. Polarized, maybe."

After a few minutes with a torch, Sid popped the *Valkyrie*'s cockpit and poked his head in. A moment later he sat up, rubbing at the nape of his neck. "I think you should come down here, Brother Perseus."

"Lucien, keep things together for a moment?"

"Take your time. Describe the smell for me."

Percy dropped the *Archer* to one knee, so that a short hop took him to the riverbank. Sid held down a hand and hauled him onto the *Valkyrie*'s back. He motioned to the gaping hole in the 'Mech's head. Percy was inured to death from an early age. His mind compartmentalized it, shunted all the horror into a corner and let him work unhindered, but what he found in the cockpit twanged his nerves like a bowstring. At first he had the same reaction as Sid, sitting up and scratching his head. Sid looked at him as if to say *I told you.*

"This was sealed from the inside?"

"*Aff.* Been in this river for years, by the look of things, but not a drop of water has penetrated it. The air is stale."

Percy took a second look inside the cockpit and beheld the emptiness of it. Nothing looked damaged. The neurohelmet rested neatly fastened on its shelf behind the command couch, and all the sensors and wiring for the MechWarrior's cooling vest were properly stowed. Percy lowered himself as far into the cockpit as he could without falling. The cut edge he gripped was still warm, but inside the *Valkyrie*'s head, his breath steamed. Of Thaddeus MacEoghan there was no sign, save the residue of death. A wide streak of dried blood as thick as paint began on the left side of the command couch, slid down across the floor, up the adjoining console, and onto the ferroglass. There, it hit a divider in the glass and simply stopped. Nothing else remained, not even a stray hair on the neurohelmet.

A touch of cold entered Percy's bones, a touch of the grave. Nothing here was right. He'd spent a lifetime seeking out the unusual, but finding it left an entirely new chill in him. Hauling himself back into the noonday sun did little to relieve it. "Find a suitable place to make camp, and radio these coordinates to the ship. They can salvage the 'Mech at their leisure. We'll hold a service for Brother Thaddeus at sundown."

Idania's voice crackled in his earpiece. "Do we have anything we can bring back to his family?"

"I don't know. I just know he won't be coming home."

As the sun set, Percy conducted a brief service for their fallen brother. Sid and most of his infantry attended, standing in respectful silence to observe the sendoff of a warrior. Lucien Clearwater remained aloof, scanning the prairie in his *White Raven.*

"He still has a Trueborn's disdain," said Sid, joining Percy in frowning at the birdlike 'Mech silhouetted in the twilight. "A few more years among the freeborn and *solahma,* and he will lose it. Or die of it."

"I need him to come down here and tell me if what we saw on Brother Thaddeus' 'Mech is the same as what your Watch has encountered before."

"It is."

"You've seen it?"

"*Neg.*" Sid lifted his chin toward Lucien's 'Mech. "But this find troubles the Red Raven. When a man who laughs at life grows somber, we must all be wary. I have opened many BattleMech cockpits. Even the worst of them had something dead to remove."

Pritchard sat nearby, reviewing holos of the scans he'd made of MacEoghan's *Valkyrie*. He scoffed at Sid's words. "I can go on the local holonet right now and find you a dozen magicians who can escape from a 'Mech cockpit and leave it locked from the inside. Welded shut, even. The mystery here isn't how, just who."

Percy pointed out scarred armor on the holographic *Valkyrie*. "What caused that damage pattern?"

"A PPC, but that means nothing. There are 'Mechs all over the surrounding fiefs that could have done this."

"If a fiefdom had done this, then the 'Mech would be in their hangar right now, not face down in a river. It was left here for a reason."

Idania walked up, still wearing her cooling vest in the warm night. "Maybe that reason was to be found, and by people specifically looking for it. This was a message, and I don't like its meaning. We've got what we came here for. We should back off."

"Finding Brother Thaddeus is only half of our mission. We still don't know how or why he died, or who is responsible."

"We know who you want it to be," Pritchard said. "Just don't kill us trying to prove it." He and Idania wandered off together. They were growing very close of late.

Percy caught Sid looking amused. "What are you smiling at?"

"You let them get away with much. If I questioned Lucien Clearwater like that, I would fall in a Circle of Equals."

"I value their opinions. Sometimes that means letting them talk. If they step out of line, I'll put them back in place." He looked out into the darkness, wondering what stared back. "What do *you* think is out there?"

Sid folded his arms. "Trouble."

PARSON LANDHOLD
NOVO FRANKLIN
THE PERIPHERY
6 JULY 3151

There was little left but ash, and the skeletons of what had once been a thriving complex. All was quiet and still amid the charred walls and collapsed roofs of Parson's farm. Dense fog blanketed the ground, enveloping their 'Mechs. There might have been a sun, but they also may have passed from the realm of the living into purgatory, to interrogate the dead.

Pritchard scanned the ruins in his *Fire Javelin*, picking what he could from the skeletons of homes, barns, and warehouses. "This wasn't a natural fire. The burn patterns say it blazed hot but went out quickly. Must have been raining when this happened. Which means an accelerant was used."

"Inferno rounds?" Percy asked.

"No. Those leave chemical residue. I'd guess flamers." A pause. "Last I checked, *Marauder*s don't mount flamers."

Percy raised his *Archer*'s arms, each sporting two Clan-grade lasers. "Modifications happen. I'm going down for a closer look. Idania, with me."

The ground had hardened into a dried, cracked cake. The night of the fire was the last time it had seen rain. Idania wandered among the wreckage, arms held close over her cooling vest. She would find what she would find. Percy had already seen what he wanted: a single, pristine track, stamped into the mud outside the main house. Four toes, two in front, two in back. He took out his tape and began to measure.

Idania wandered over. She had found something, a child's toy of some kind, which she turned over and over in her hands. She watched as Percy measured the distance between two toes and scribbled in his notebook. "What do you hope to find by doing that?"

Percy snapped the book shut. "This track is four point seven meters long. The footprint of a *Marauder* out of Kathil is four point two-five meters, on average. There will be variation depending on the vagaries of the environment, but not this much."

"Maybe it's the big brother 'Mech, the *Marauder II*? Or maybe it isn't a *Marauder* at all?"

"Maybe one of you would shut up and trust me. Just once."

Idania turned away, biting her lip.

Percy felt his color rise. "I'm sorry."

She nodded her forgiveness, but said softly, "Obsession is dangerous, Percy."

"I know that. I didn't choose you and Pritchard at random. I trust you to let me know when it gets out of hand. And I promise to listen." He looked around at the wreckage of the Parson farm. "Besides, we have a duty to bring justice to the people who died here, no matter who was responsible."

"Maybe we can help with that." Sid and one of his troopers approached, carrying between them a ragged, filthy man. They dropped him at Percy's feet. "Found him in the big house, curled up on a burnt mattress."

"Why is he bleeding?"

Sid shrugged. "He tried to run."

Percy bent over the man, who cringed and shielded his eyes. He was barely a man at all. No razor had yet touched his cheeks. His skin was coated with a layer of dirt and rubbed-in ash. Most striking, his hair was growing in white; a centimeter showed at the roots.

"What happened here?" Percy asked, but the boy merely mumbled. "What was that?"

"Good boy," Sid said, and Percy looked at him sharply. "He's saying 'good boy.' It was all we got out of him."

Percy looked to Idania. Hers was the gentlest soul, and she took his meaning. She put her arms around the boy and held him while Percy fetched a canteen and some rations. The mechanical stomping of Lucien Clearwater's 'Mech somewhere in the mist seemed to grow agitated the longer they tarried. He clearly wanted to move on from this place of death, but there were yet secrets to wring from the bones.

It took a long time for the boy to speak, in clipped syllables and nods. Most of what he said was the same repetitive mumbling of "Good boy...good boy..." Eventually Idania drew out that his name was Kenji, and the Parson farm had been his home.

Percy squatted beside Idania and the boy. "I have to ask him some difficult questions now."

"I wish it weren't so. Death has taken his mind. Time may give it back, but the mark will never leave. He has no past to return to. It's all ashes now. Do it gently, Percy."

"Kenji? Kenji, look at me."

He did, but stared at a point somewhere on Percy's chin. "Good...good boy..."

"Yes, you are. Can you tell me who did this to your home?"

Kenji's bottom lip trembled. "God. It was God. He's mean. He killed them all. But I'm a good boy. I show respect."

"God doesn't do things like this," Idania whispered. "It was people."

Kenji just shook his head, and kept shaking it. Idania shushed him and held him close.

Percy clasped the boy's arm and pulled him firmly around. Idania scowled at him, but he ignored her. "Why did God do this? No, Kenji, don't cry. You're stronger than that. You're still alive. Help me understand. Why?"

"Thou shalt not have false idols...nor imitate the face of God..."

"Nor steal, nor kill, nor commit adultery." Percy knew the litany of commandments and sins, and all the other things he was not supposed to do. None of them were of help as his patience began to slip. "Was it another fief? Or pirates, the mudfoots? Did they make demands your master wouldn't meet, and did they do this in retaliation?"

For the first time, the boy looked him in the eye. His gaze was puzzled, but completely lucid. "The mudfoots were our friends. We fed them, took care of their 'Mechs." He pointed to one of the larger ruins. It looked big enough to have housed BattleMechs. "They fought Master Parson's enemies, brought us booty. Lots of things."

"Like this?" Idania held up the toy she had found.

Sid and the other Elemental laughed fondly when they saw it. "Khan Polly." Sid took it and turned it over. "Raven manufacture. This would not be available outside one of our enclaves."

"How did it get here, Kenji?"

"For the children...always something for the children. They could grow up to be mudfoots one day. But that was wrong. That was our sin."

"No arguing that," Idania mumbled. "Did the mudfoots have names?"

"Reese...Mifune...Apple Barrel, the one with the robot leg... Hot-top... The leader, Langstrom..."

Percy's head snapped up. A great fire shot up his spine as every hair stood on edge. Idania's mouth hung open. Her eyes met his, and she shook her head slightly, not in disbelief, but in denial. Percy's smile was the savage righteousness of vindication, but he tamped it back down. His faith was absolute, but faith is not fact. He needed more.

"I'm going to show you some pictures, Kenji. Tell me if any of them look familiar." Percy displayed some still holos from Defiance. A *Brigand*; a *Quickdraw*; a *Shadow Hawk*. None of them drew a reaction. Percy clicked to the last image.

The boy shrieked, suddenly and loudly enough that Sid and his partner raised their guns in alarm. Kenji scuttled backward like a crab, one arm shielding his face. "I'm a good boy! Good boy!" He prostrated himself on the ground before the graven image, turning it to mud with his tears. "I show respect! I bow to the lord!"

In Percy's hand, the holographic image of Kevin Langstrom's *Marauder* seemed to grin.

The comm squawked in Pritchard's voice. "Get in your 'Mechs! We have incoming!"

Percy swore. The Devil always lurked nearby to throw a wrench in the works.

They ran, leaving Kenji to vanish back into the ruins. That poor soul would have to fend for himself.

Percy saw shapes moving far off in the mist. He donned his neurohelmet just as a series of red dots lit up his HUD. His gut leaped. Seven, eight, nine... They kept coming, 'Mechs as black as tar, splotched with red as if spattered with the blood of their victims. His HUD labeled them one by one. *Grand Dragon*, *Guillotine*, *Dervish*, *Blackjack*. With them came off-road trucks full of screaming mudfoots hanging out the doors and howling like animals.

"We are outnumbered and outmaneuvered," Lucien Clearwater said. "Much as it pains me, a tactical advance to the rear is in order."

The *Grand Dragon* loosed a flight of LRMs, which hammered into the soil between their 'Mechs. Lucien's *White Raven* raised its arms. "A parting gift, shall we?"

Percy triggered his own LRMs. Lucien's deadly accurate lasers hit the *Dragon* seconds before forty missiles engulfed it in a fiery cloud. The pirate 'Mech collapsed and did not rise.

Pritchard's *Fire Javelin* twitched. "They're flanking us! Trying to herd us south. I'll bet there's a surprise waiting there."

"Can't be worse than what's up front." Percy toggled his deep LRM bays to Thunder munitions, which would scatter mines wherever they landed. Minefields were a despicable weapon that didn't discriminate between friend, foe, or innocent, but they had their uses. The Thunder missiles peppered the ground once trod by Parson's cattle. Some of the black 'Mechs saw where his shots landed and paused. "I think I can buy us some time. Pritchard! See what's to the south."

Mist swirled like smoke as missiles and particle beams soared across Parson's fields. Percy held down the trigger of his LRMs, alternating between standard munitions and Thunder missiles. Two of his ammo bins ran dry, but he had plenty more. He fired a flight of fragmentation ammo at the howling trucks of fools, muttering a prayer for those it caught. A *Locust* and a *Scarabus*, small but deadly-fast 'Mechs, raced down the western edge, trying to flank them.

Idania's *Chameleon* was traditionally a training 'Mech, but it also made an excellent bug hunter. Percy didn't need to order her. She jumped into the path of the smaller machines and pierced the *Locust*'s hide with a beam from her large laser. The gangly 'Mech drove into the ground, plowing rich dirt ahead of it. The *Scarabus* dodged Idania's secondary fire and sprayed her torso and legs with lasers of its own. Her second volley sent it running back to its companions.

"South is no good!" Pritchard's voice was an octave above normal. "I counted five more hostiles. How many of these guys are there?"

At least fourteen, and they were closing in like the jaws of a predator. The black *Dervish* answered Percy's LRM fire even as he retreated. His Thunder-missile minefields downed one 'Mech, but mines couldn't be relied on forever. If he and his companions couldn't extract themselves soon, the enemy would crush them under the sheer weight of their numbers.

"We're clear to the east!" Lucien shouted. His *White Raven* stood over the smoking hulks of two enemy 'Mechs and a pair of hovercraft, laser scars marring its red paint. "Sid, cover our retreat."

Percy ordered them out. Sid's two Anat APCs rolled past him in the opposite direction as Idania's *Chameleon* caught up.

"They're going to die," Idania said as her 'Mech slowed.

"They want to," Percy said somberly. "Pray for them, but don't deny them their last wish."

Gray-haired warriors hung from the Anats' open doors, ready to jump out and engage the enemy one last time. The lead Anat rammed headlong into one of the pursuing trucks full of mudfoots, disintegrating the civilian vehicle on impact and scattering twisted metal and bodies to the wind. The second Anat disgorged its cargo at the feet of the black *Guillotine*, and Percy felt a rush of awe as Sid's infantry scrambled up the 70-ton 'Mech with satchel charges slung over their shoulders and knives clenched between their teeth. Percy was in no hurry to die, but when the Lord called him home, he hoped he could muster just a fraction of this bravery.

"Mary, Joseph, and the blessed Baby Jesus!" The fear in Idania's voice slinked through Percy's earpiece and threatened to infect his brain. He pushed his *Archer*'s throttle harder, and as he rounded a copse of trees, he saw what had driven her to it.

Cloaked in otherworldly gray was a shadow as dark as a hole in reality. It was as if something had stepped into this world from a place beyond the ether and taken a form that suited it. A form inhuman and disconcerting. Mist swirled around its feet, as though it trod on something other than the mortal earth. Percy's scanners confirmed what his eyes saw.

Marauder.

"Randis," crackled a voice over an open frequency. It was mechanical, synthesized. Those bulky, blocky arms raised in his direction. Flanking it like a pair of zombie servants were twin *Crusader*s, one with its head and shoulders painted in shining gold, the other in burnished copper. They trained forearms laden with LRMs on Percy and Idania.

Percy's heart felt like a sledgehammer inside his chest. He gasped for air inside his neurohelmet. There it was! After so many long years and countless rumors, he had found it, confirmed it.

The Dark One had returned, with a Langstrom at its controls.

And he, Perseus Schell, was badly outmatched.

Idania stood beside him, but Lucien and Pritchard were too far away, and the *Marauder* had allies closing in. LRMs landed between him and Idania, peppering both 'Mechs. He returned fire, not knowing what he hit, and unconsciously pushed his *Archer* forward.

"Percy, we have to go!" Idania shouted, but he ignored her. He pressed on, loosing more missiles as the black 'Mechs responded in kind. A dreamlike glaze came over him, and all he knew was to advance and shoot, and damn the cost.

"Percy, it's out of hand! *It's out of hand right now!*"

He blinked, and gasped for breath. The thrill in his spine turned cold. The enemy closed from three sides now, just entering long range. Lasers and high-speed autocannon rounds *zing*ed by. There would be no justice if he died here.

He began to back off. "Idania, go! I'll cover."

He switched back to Thunder munitions and laid mines in front of the *Marauder* and *Crusader*s he could barely see through mist and smoke, and prayed the Lord would fell them. He sent two flights each toward the other advancing forces and followed Idania east. Every step was like waking from a nightmare into bleak reality.

FORTY KILOMETERS EAST OF PARSON LANDHOLD

They ran for most of the day, and finally came to a series of rolling hills, where they took shelter in a deep hollow. Pritchard noted no pursuit. They pitched a camp in silence while Lucien Clearwater stood guard.

A few hours later, Sid rolled up with half his squad and one badly damaged APC. The survivors were extraordinarily jovial and broke out a case of whiskey as they relived the battle and the deeds of companions now gone. Sid reported the black 'Mechs were not following, but had dug in to occupy the ruins.

It wasn't a particularly cool night, but Percy shivered under his blanket, clutching a hot cup of coffee. He did not refuse when Sid offered him something stronger. The infantry built themselves a bonfire a short distance from Percy's little stove, segregating themselves from the MechWarriors as tradition often demanded, and proceeded to hold a loud party. Sid abstained, saying they had earned a celebration, but he had not.

Pritchard collected the battleROMs from their 'Mechs for review. Sid sat with him, sharing observations about the enemy's behavior and conferring on tactics for defeating individual 'Mechs. Idania said nothing for a long time, sipping the drink Sid gave her and staring pensively into the distance. Percy watched her and waited. Idania's mind pieced information together in a wholly unique way, leading her to conclusions he often missed.

"Something isn't right," she finally said.

Percy looked up. "A lot of things weren't right today."

She continued as if he hadn't spoken. "Why did they come back? What did they have left to gain from that place?"

"Did they come back?" Lucien Clearwater had finally come down from his 'Mech, a holovid ideal with his whipcord-tight muscles, his blond hair gently fluttering in the breeze. "Or did they never leave? That farm made for an effective ambush point."

"You think they knew we were coming?" Pritchard asked.

Lucien shrugged. "We have been shadowed ever since we set foot on this planet."

Percy's head snapped up. "You're just now sharing this?"

"They have kept their distance. Barely a blip on my sensors, and sometimes not even that. Just a feeling. I assumed it was a scout for one of the fiefs. I think differently now." Lucien took a swig from one of Sid's bottles and sighed contentedly. "It is not there tonight. I may finally get a good night's rest."

Idania looked unsatisfied. If anything, her frown had deepened. "These mudfoots raid off-world. That toy I found proves that. But where is their DropShip?"

"Hidden somewhere distant," Pritchard said. "I'll bet good money Parson wasn't the only one who harbored them, both on and off Novo Franklin. If he wasn't their only hidey-hole, then they wouldn't have a problem burning him out if he pissed them off somehow."

"Langstrom was Federated Suns-trained." Percy felt their skeptical eyes but didn't care. "He would know how to counter pirate-hunting tactics."

"Percy," Pritchard said slowly. "Kevin Langstrom would be over a hundred years old by now."

"The oldest woman on Randis IV is one hundred and fifteen, and she's still sharper than most." Frustrated, he sighed. "Maybe I'm not right, but that boy at the Parson farm gave me a name, and that name was Langstrom. You all saw the *Marauder*."

"We saw *a Marauder*," Idania said. "It gave me a start, but it didn't seem unusual. It didn't feel like...well, like that dagger you have."

"It gave me a chill," Pritchard said. "Or maybe it was its dozen buddies."

Percy gritted his teeth. They were being so damn stubborn. He took out his little notebook to review what he had about Kevin Langstrom and the Dark One, but found his thoughts unwilling to focus. There was nothing in his notes he hadn't already memorized.

"Why do you use that old thing?" Lucien Clearwater asked.

"Writing comforts me. Besides, I hope to publish it all one day, and no one can hack a notebook."

"Can't wait to read it," Pritchard said. "*Brother Percy's Catalog of the Absurd, Abnormal, and Unusual, Periphery Edition*."

"The unusual surrounds us, but you're too inured to realize it." Percy closed his little book and looked at Pritchard. "We got here by ripping a hole in the fabric of space-time and shoving ourselves through it. That doesn't seem abnormal to you? Humanity's been tinkering with jump drives for a thousand years, and we still don't understand how they work. They just do, and we don't question why."

"Fourth-dimensional space," Lucien said. "Jump drives utilize fourth-dimensional space."

Pritchard squinted at him. "You mean time? The fourth dimension is time."

"No, I mean another spatial dimension beyond our three." Lucien looked around at a field of blank stares. "Do you learn nothing in your backwater schools?"

Percy perused his notebook. "I have something on higher dimensions in here. I thought it was all conjecture?"

"No, it's fact. I'd know more if I'd been a WarShip captain, but all Snow Ravens learn a little bit in our *sibko* years." Lucien pointed to the night sky. "All of that is curved. Whichever direction you travel, you end up back where you started. Always. The only way this is possible is if our three-dimensional universe exists on the surface of a fourth-dimensional object."

Idania rubbed the bridge of her nose. "I don't think I'm drunk enough for this conversation."

The Red Raven laughed. "Let me take it down a step. Say you were as flat as that pancake Pritchard calls a nose." He scribbled a letter *P* in the dirt. "All you would perceive is left, right, forward, and back. There is no up or down. You see only flatness. Now if you were to walk…" He drew a line from the *P* out as far as he could reach and continued pointing to the horizon. "Straight in a line, never moving left or right, you would eventually arrive right back here." He jammed the tip of his blade into the center of his two-dimensional Pritchard. "You would have no concept of the curvature of the planet because you cannot perceive it. Yet, because you have gotten back to where you began, you can deduce the existence of that curvature. The same applies to hyperspace. We know that a higher spatial dimension exists because our three-dimensional universe curves around it."

They all stared at Lucien's drawing for a moment, then Pritchard took a big drink. Idania and Percy followed suit. It was brain-bending, but interesting. Percy made a note to get a better description from Lucien later to enter into his journal.

"Don't pass out yet, it gets stranger." Lucien prodded his two-dimensional Pritchard. "This ugly little fellow cannot see us because we are above him, in the third dimension. He could only perceive the sliver of us that intersects his plane, if we choose to intersect it at all." He stamped a boot print into the dirt. "There. That is all he would see of me. That print, and only from the side. A line, really. That is all he sees of me, but I can see the entirety of him, even his insides. I can perceive his entire two-dimensional reality all at once. If I chose to, I could pluck him right out of his dimension, remove him completely from his plane of existence, like that." He snapped his fingers. "Then I can replace him anywhere, at any spot. I can place him inside a locked building or remove him from one. I can put him into a different two-dimensional plane, a similar but separate reality to his own. Using the third dimension, I can do all sorts of things that he wouldn't even believe were possible, because he lacks the ability to think three-dimensionally.

"*That* is how hyperspace works. For a brief moment, we hop into a higher dimension—fourth-dimensional space—and hop out again at a place we could never have gotten to without it."

Pritchard swallowed. "Your little two-D me there. If you plucked him up...would he know what was happening to him?"

"You mean would he perceive an intelligent hand in his misery?" Lucien shrugged. "He would see a sliver. Likewise, a fourth-dimensional entity would appear to us as a sliver. We could not recognize it for what it was. Our brains could only perceive it three-dimensionally, and for our own sanity would inflict on it a shape our minds could recognize."

Chills ran up Percy's spine. "Any shape?"

"I suppose, if the effort were put in."

Pritchard's eyebrows rose. "'Mech-shaped, Percy? Is that where you're going?"

The foolishness of it all rushed in at him. Pritchard seemed just on the verge of laughter, and Idania wore a patronizing look. Lucien Clearwater had set him up for this, but the Red Raven was not laughing. He just slowly sipped his drink.

Percy's face flushed. "Forget it. I'm getting drunk."

Idania shook her head. "Why do you hate that 'Mech so much, Percy? Black Kevin Langstrom disappeared seventy years ago. What could he have possibly done to you?"

"Defiance," Percy said.

Pritchard scoffed. "This is all because of your stubborn will?"

"Not the act, the world. Defiance, in the Suns' Outback. It's my home planet."

Idania had her pad out. "Langstrom hit Defiance in 3080. Over a thousand casualties, and millions of D-bills in damage. They didn't even rob anything major, just a few banks. Petty theft."

"It wasn't what he took, it's what he left behind. Langstrom met my grandmother on that day."

Lucien Clearwater spat out his drink. "Don't tell me anything disgusting about Spheroid breeding."

"No, not like that. She was already pregnant with my mother. Langstrom didn't hurt her much at all, not physically. He just used her as a human shield. Chained her across the Dark One's PPC barrel, daring any Defiance defender to make him fire."

"Jesus, Mary, and Joseph." Pritchard crossed himself. "I guess she survived?"

"Somehow. Somehow in the hours he spent tearing up the city, he never fired that weapon. It was a miracle, or maybe it was his plan. She survived, but she was never the same, so I'm told. My mother shielded me from her, only let me see her a handful of times." Percy rubbed his brow, trying to massage out the painful memories. "My grandmother was cold, serpent-like. Dead behind the eyes. Her brothers told me she only became that way after Langstrom."

None of Percy's companions had anything to say, but now, perhaps, they understood. Langstrom had disappeared, giving no closure to the families he had ruined. There was no noble House Schell to seek vengeance, only Perseus, his *Archer*, and whichever companions would follow him. And maybe, just maybe, he might not get them all killed chasing ghosts.

FORTY KILOMETERS EAST OF PARSON LANDHOLD
NOVO FRANKLIN
THE PERIPHERY
7 JULY 3151

Percy awoke to a toe shoving him through the side of his tent. Lucien Clearwater stood outside, in full gear. "Come with me, Perseus. I want to check something."

The hour was late. A few infantrymen sat dull-faced and silent around the fire, and Idania stood overwatch in her *Chameleon.* Sluggish and grumbling, Percy dressed and donned his cooling vest, but Lucien stopped him halfway to his *Archer.*

"Don't bring that old beater. Come ride with me."

BattleMechs were never made to accommodate passengers, but most sported a rumble seat for emergencies. Percy rarely had occasion to be grateful for his short stature, but it made squeezing in behind the *White Raven*'s command couch simpler. He found it surprisingly cozy, even if he did have to sit sideways. Lucien would never have fit back here.

"Why are we doing this?" Percy asked as Lucien slipped in and sealed the cockpit.

"There are things I want to tell you, but I don't want your associates to hear. Or mine. I am not even sure I should tell you, but I trust you more than most. I guess that's why they call me crazy." Lucien powered up the 'Mech and uttered his security phrase: "*In vino veritas.*"

They rode in silence for a long time. Lucien would speak when he was ready. Percy thought of him as a friend, but was never certain if that sentiment was really returned. The mind of a Clanner was hard to know. The mind of a Clanner many thought insane?

Instead, Percy focused on the *White Raven,* marveling at its efficiency. His *Archer* was ancient, and smelled of every MechWarrior who'd ever pissed themself in its pilot seat. People had lived out of that 'Mech. This one lacked the amenities necessary for such a life. It was a sleek tool of war, a reflection of its pilot.

The eastern sky purpled. Percy stretched as best he could, massaging his legs. "Where are we?"

Lucien let out a minor and very fake cry. "Oh! I forgot you were there."

Percy slapped him on the back of his neurohelmet.

"We are nearly back to the Parson farm."

"What?" Percy jolted up and banged his head.

"Relax. They are too stupid to set a proper guard." All playfulness departed. For the moment, Lucien was a typical Clan warrior. "I wanted another look. And, if possible, your opinion."

In moments, the crumbled outbuildings of the Parson landhold appeared on Lucien's long-range infrared scanners. Tiny heat blips marked the spot of BattleMechs in standby. None blazed with the fire of a fully powered-up machine.

"Brasher warriors than we two wise men would rush in and try to take them while they sleep," Lucien said. Percy silently prayed Lucien would not lose his wisdom. Lucien shut down his IR sensors and gazed out through the cockpit ferroglass. "Look out there, Brother, and tell me what you see."

Percy struggled into a position to see the farm. There was no fog this morning. "A burned-out wreck, and a bunch of black 'Mechs. We should have brought Pritchard's 'Mech. Its sensors are better."

Lucien began to circle the farm. "There are things our 'Mechs cannot see. *That* is something you need to know. But here I think it does not apply." He switched his computer back on. "My targeting computer is as good as your ugly friend's sensors. Let's see what it sees."

Tags appeared over each greenish blip on the IR scanner. *Stinger. Shadow Hawk. Rokurokubi.*

Marauder.

"Is that what you're looking for?" Lucien asked.

Percy's heart pumped. He'd seen it on his scanners not twenty-four hours ago, studied the grainy battleROM image that told him little beyond it being a *Marauder*, painted jet black. "Can we get closer?"

Lucien smiled brightly. "Of course!"

"Lucien! Don't!" Percy braced himself as the *White Raven* throttled up to maximum. He watched Lucien power up his lasers, and said a prayer to the Savior and the Blessed Virgin.

The *White Raven* barreled directly for the largest 'Mech, a squat, blocky *Warlord*. Lucien waited until nearly point-blank range before triggering his lasers, placing all of them with frightening accuracy on the *Warlord*'s left hip. The joint exploded, and Percy felt the rumble as 80 tons of crippled BattleMech crashed to the earth. The cockpit grew uncomfortably warm, and Percy's cooling vest was not connected. He fumbled with the auxiliary hoses as Lucien jerked the 'Mech around.

Small-arms fire pinged off the canopy. The mudfoots were quick to react but ineffective. Lucien raked them with his pulse lasers. "What say you, Brother Perseus? Should we take another?"

Several shapes raced up their chain ladders in the predawn. A few of the black 'Mechs had already started moving.

"Get us out of here before you get us killed!" Percy shouted.

"How about the little one?" Lucien's large lasers tore through the center of the pirate *Stinger*, collapsing it into a heap of scrap.

A particle blast smacked one of the *Raven*'s gangly arms. "*Lucien!*"

Cackling with far too much glee, Lucien turned and raced away. Sweat dripped off Percy's nose, and his hands shook. He'd never wanted to hit someone so badly in his life.

Lucien looked over his shoulder, saw Percy's face, and lost his smile. "Don't go losing your religion on me now, Brother. I'm driving." Long-range missiles slammed into the *White Raven*'s rear. "Aw, they're not happy to see us go. Just sit tight. I can outshoot what I can't outrun."

In a short amount of time, he had outrun them. The pirates chose to count their losses, maybe hunker down in Parson's ashes and wait for an assault that wasn't coming. Percy silently seethed, trying his best not to look at Lucien Clearwater. He couldn't argue with the results of the man's impulsive raid, but the unexpected risk to his own life galled him. The helplessness of it all.

Lucien found a small, wooded dip in the plains with a quiet brook at the bottom and parked his 'Mech. "I need a piss. Let's stretch our legs."

Percy walked a good distance away and splashed cold, wild water on his face. Lucien filtered a liter of it and handed Percy a fresh canteen. "Once your anger wears off, we should talk."

"That will probably be next year."

"Well, let's do it now, then." Lucien held out a holoprojector and displayed the battleROM from their misadventure. Percy watched the silent insanity play out in double speed. Lucien froze the playback a moment after the *Warlord* fell, displaying a crisp capture of the black *Marauder*.

"Why couldn't you have shot that one?" Percy said.

"Why? Take a closer look, Perseus. That is not the 'Mech of Kevin Langstrom."

"How can you be so sure?"

"Because I can see it," Lucien said. Something deep and frightening lurked in his words. He stared at Percy's blank face for a moment, then snarled, "Compare it to your own holo from Defiance."

Percy had left that holo back at camp, but he did not need it. He'd long ago memorized every bizarre angle, every unexpected curve and bulge of the Dark One, Black Kevin's sadistic BattleMech. He hated that this 'Mech did not match. It was black, but it clearly had classic General Motors *Marauder* lines.

Percy suddenly felt very tired. He drained his canteen, then stripped off his boots and lay down on the bank to soak his feet in the cold, rushing water. "I feel like you could have done this with holos we already had from yesterday."

Lucien sighed. "I told you there were things I wanted you to know. My Clan, in its wisdom, does not share information easily. It is a Snow Raven failing. My superiors would demote me to dead if they learned I told you anything."

"But you haven't told me anything."

That earned Percy a slap on the head. "Unimaginative slug. You can't wrap your thick head around subtlety." Lucien rubbed his eyes. "Fine. But remember, I hold you in confidence. None of this gets to anyone else, or I'll kill you."

Percy smiled wryly. "Before or after your superiors kill you?"

"Both." Lucien leaned back on his haunches. "Events in the Republic of the Sphere are coming to a head. Great changes may be afoot, but they do not concern us."

"Then why bring it up?"

"Because those events are keeping Snow Raven eyes focused inward. Some of us, namely those thrown out into it, think the Periphery bears closer watching. Pirate activity in the Wastes has changed. The Dark Caste is organizing, becoming more efficient. Someone is promoting a wider agenda than just their next raid."

A pulsating pain began behind Percy's eye. The Grand Knight wouldn't be happy to hear of a new bandit kingdom coalescing in the Outworlds Wastes. The Brotherhood had enough trouble dealing with Tortuga. Percy would have to share this with them, regardless of Lucien's confidence.

"The Raven Watch is stretched thin," Lucien continued. "Every time we have tried to investigate, we die. We can only spare small forces, like the Star your Brotherhood heard about. That was Onverwacht, in the Wastes. We suspect it to be the epicenter. None of our people ever survive, but sometimes there are other witnesses. One commonality is the presence of a *Marauder*, black as the soul of Stefan Amaris."

Percy looked at Lucien's frozen holo. "This one looks very black."

"Indeed." Lucien sounded disappointed.

They sat in silence for a time, enjoying the serenity of their little glade. Eventually Lucien stood and brushed himself off. "Our companions must think us dead. Better go disappoint them."

He hauled Percy to his feet and clasped his shoulder. "That 'Mech is not the object of your obsession, Brother Perseus, but do not drop your guard. Frightening and dangerous things exist in the Spinward drifts, and they can come unexpectedly. For now, let us have fun smashing these *dezgra* fools."

CARLTON DRAW
NOVO FRANKLIN
THE PERIPHERY
12 JULY 3151

The trap was Pritchard's idea. He spent hours poring over grainy terrain photos to find a place advantageous enough for them to face three-to-one odds. Sid praised his choice, commenting he would do well in the Clan trial system.

The Carlton Draw ran along the path of an ancient riverbed. Its high walls created a sharp ridge line overlooking a maze of sandstone pillars, providing ambush points and kill zones aplenty. Luring the enemy there would be the easy part, as the pirates had chased them every day since Lucien's ill-begotten raid.

Following the tread of BattleMechs across soft prairie earth was never difficult. Black 'Mechs appeared just on the edge of scanning range, reminding them of the odds they faced. The group could only travel as fast as their slowest 'Mech, Percy's *Archer.* He constantly expected to be overrun, but even the faster pirate 'Mechs kept their distance. Langstrom liked for his prey to know fear. Despite that *Marauder* not being the Dark One, a niggle of doubt never left Percy's soul.

They had mere hours to prepare the Draw. Percy laid his last few Thunder minefields at choke points, while Sid's infantry dug hasty foxholes nearby, ready to spring out and finish any downed 'Mechs. Idania and Pritchard practiced a bait and switch, where Pritchard's *Fire Javelin* would lure enemies into the close-range guns of Idania's *Chameleon.* Percy found a long stretch of open ground, where his *Archer* could command the field from a narrow gap. Anyone wanting to challenge him would have to march down his alley of fire.

Lucien remained their ace. His 'Mech was the most powerful, and he could outmaneuver and outshoot them all. He might not even need their help. Percy tried to include him in their plans, but the Red Raven had become surly again. A warrior among soldiers, Lucien Clearwater would fight his own battle.

The enemy waited until night, when a nasty storm whipped up fierce winds, and blue lightning blazed across a fortress of clouds. Perhaps they thought their 'Mechs would disappear into a cloak of darkness, or perhaps this Langstrom just liked the weather.

There were fewer of them than Percy expected. Nine black 'Mechs walked into the Draw, many showing signs of damage from their previous engagement. Where were the rest? Were they playing it smart and holding a force in reserve? Did they send jumpers to reach the top of the ridge and fire down? The answers waited in the sandstone pillars and crags, to be drawn out by fire and death.

"We aren't going to run anymore," Percy broadcast. "This is a good place to die. We are at peace with our Lord and savior. I urge you to surrender, so that your souls, too, may be saved."

No response.

Percy shrugged. The offer was just a formality. No one would be surrendering here tonight.

It began when the gold-accented *Crusader* triggered one of Percy's minefields. The 'Mech staggered, but did not fall. It seemed to grow angry, then triggered its jump jets and rocketed over the spot. The rest of the black 'Mechs did not advance cautiously, but crowded through the gap. Some jumped, and some crossed the minefield safely. Only a *Centurion* fell, to be immediately swarmed by Sid's infantry.

Percy did not have a direct line of sight, but received a feed from Pritchard's 'Mech. The *Fire Javelin* raced from cover to blast its lasers into the clot of enemies, then jumped back along the route leading to Idania's ambush point. Two 'Mechs pursued, but Percy couldn't identify them. He tried to focus on finding the *Marauder*. Kill the leader, kill the unit.

The enemy spread out into the Draw, displaying a lack of discipline and cohesion. None were trained soldiers. Each mudfoot fought alone, and that would make them easier to kill. Explosions and lasers lit the night, and on the occasions when lightning flashed, Percy saw a jumping 'Mech frozen in the sky as if in a single still holo.

Panicked chatter on the open channel told him Lucien Clearwater had joined the fray.

Percy took a step out of his narrow gap to survey his killing field. "Pritchard, Idania, fall back! Bring them to me!"

A few tense minutes later, they emerged at the far end, skirting the minefield laid there. Pritchard's 'Mech was missing an arm and limped horribly. Idania's *Chameleon* had a hole in its right torso where half of its guns use to be.

Percy's finger hovered over his LRM trigger. "How many of them are still standing?"

"A hundred?" Pritchard offered.

"Be serious."

"No," Idania said. "I think a hundred is accurate."

"Clearwater took down the *Dervish*," Pritchard said as he limped past Percy. "And Sid got another one. The rest have taken some hits, but they're righteously pissed off now!"

"Any sign of the *Marauder*?"

"It's there," Idania said. "Right in the middle. It hit Lucien a couple of times before he jumped away."

A moment later, Percy saw for himself. Lightning revealed movement at the mouth of his open pit. The *Crusader* walked through with arms raised, and behind it came two more shadows. One was a *Corvis*, a former Snow Raven 'Mech. The other, a classic General Motors *Marauder*. Seeing it live and with an objective eye, there was no doubt. It was not the Dark One.

Somehow, this filled Percy with a disappointed rage. He took another step forward, and the *Crusader* noticed, training its bulky forearms on him. Both 'Mechs fired simultaneously, sending seventy long-range missiles across the valley. Percy's *Archer* rocked as his wireframe armor diagram lit up yellow. The *Crusader* staggered but remained standing. That pilot was amazing; no wonder the *Marauder* had chosen this one as a bodyguard. But there had been two *Crusader*s, one gold, one copper. Percy couldn't shake the feeling that the copper one would pop up in his rear arc at any second.

Then a pair of particle blasts punched his *Archer* in the solar plexus. Its heavy armor held, but the force overwhelmed its gyro, and the *Archer* fell onto its rump. Percy slammed his head and felt a tooth chip. The Lord wasn't letting him have this victory easily.

The three enemy 'Mechs raced into the valley, the *Corvis* circling left, and the black *Marauder* right. The *Crusader* marched proudly forward—right into Percy's minefield. Its damaged legs did not hold. The right leg disintegrated below the knee, and the 'Mech fell onto its face. The other two paused, giving Percy time to right himself. He fired another round of LRMs at the *Marauder*, but hit mostly sandstone. It returned fire with a full fusillade, and again Percy's *Archer* toppled. A detached part of him resolved to replace that damned gyro, if he survived.

Jump plumes flashed overhead as Pritchard and Idania raced to his aid. Their 'Mechs were lighter and more heavily damaged than their opponents, but they charged unafraid into the fray as

Percy regained his feet. Their lasers flashed, but it could never be enough. Both of them glowed in his IR scanners from engine damage and loss of heat sinks. Pritchard's *Fire Javelin* was so sluggish an *UrbanMech* could've outrun it, but still he trained his lasers on the *Corvis*. God was with him, for two of his shots lanced into the 'Mech's jutting cockpit. God also chastised him, because the *Corvis* fired its autocannon as it fell, and cleaved the lighter *Fire Javelin* in half. Percy yelled into his comm, but got no response.

Idania tried to challenge the *Marauder*, but it ignored her. She had lost her main gun and could only hit it with ineffective smaller weapons. LRMs hammered her *Chameleon*; the downed *Crusader* had propped itself on one arm to continue the fight. Growling, Percy sent two flights of missiles into the *Crusader*, ensuring the bastard would not rise again. Idania's 'Mech staggered, and the *Marauder* shoved it out of the way. The *Chameleon* slumped against the sandstone wall and slid down it like a barroom drunk with a glass jaw.

Percy squared off with the *Marauder*, watching it twitch like a living thing. A crackle of lightning illuminated them. No other sounds came from the Carlton Draw. This was almost at its end.

"*Randis.*" The word came bathed in scorn, in a feminine voice.

Percy was taken aback. "Who are you?"

"I am Black Kevin Langstrom!" The woman laughed. "Or close enough. It doesn't matter. I am become he, therefore I am he."

"You're not Kevin Langstrom, and that's not his 'Mech!"

"One *Marauder* is as good as another. The legend will make people see what I want them to see. People were crazy enough to start seeing Black Kevin before I took his name, and they'll see him centuries from now. Legends endure, and I will be a part of that. You will be just another nameless victim."

She declared an end to the parley with a blast from her PPCs. Percy stumbled. When he looked around, the *Marauder* was vanishing back into the Draw, and he almost stepped into his own minefield chasing after her. The shakes had overtaken him. He reached for calm with some sort of prayer, but nothing came to mind. He was in a maze hunting the Devil, or something close enough to him. Prayers were of no more use.

He rounded each bend with a knot in his belly, jumping at every shadow. Once he triggered his lasers thinking he had her, but it was only a convenient outcrop of rock.

Laughter filled his comm. "Try again, Randis."

Percy needed to keep her talking. "Why impersonate Langstrom? Why not be the next Lady Death instead?"

"Paula Trevaline spent half her life in a Federat prison and died like a fool. Black Kevin was smarter. He knew the path to immortality. Be one step ahead, never get caught, and leave on your own terms. My work is worthy of his legend. You found your Brother Knight's 'Mech, yes? Sealing his cockpit from within was the easy part. The blood was my personal touch."

Percy's sensors flickered. Something was out there. "You killed a knight of the holy order. That will come with consequences."

"And you burned out Parson looking for me. Don't you think that's overreacting?"

"What?"

"The boy told us God did it. Who else goes thumping Bibles around these parts? You killed our friends and family, you hypocritical bastard! Creeping about with your sneak attacks, picking my 'Mechs off one by one, killing us as we sleep. Luring me here only after taking a third of my force."

"I don't under—"

Percy almost missed it. As he moved through the pillars, a pile of debris on his left erupted, and the *Marauder* emerged with its blocky arms raised. She was no more than thirty meters away. "Welcome to my turf, Randis. Close range, where your LRMs are worthless—"

With a savage grin, Percy unleashed forty of them. The *Marauder* disappeared under a cloud of explosions as its shots went wide. "*Clan* LRMs. Shoot first, gloat second."

Anger rose in Percy's soul as he charged forward. She had deceived him, killed one of his Brother Knights, possibly killed all of his companions. His every moment on Novo Franklin was a nightmare, and it was her fault. All her fault! And he wouldn't even get the release of destroying the Dark One, because Kevin Langstrom was long dead and faded into legend, and he, Perseus Schell, was a fool. A ghost-chasing fool leading a procession of the damned.

Percy began to beat on the *Marauder* with his 'Mech's massive fists. "You—" *Smash!* "Are not—" *Smash!* "Black—" *Smash!* "Kevin—" *Smash!* "Langstrom!"

His fist drove in an uppercut under the *Marauder*'s jutting chin, and as it made contact, Percy triggered the lasers in the *Archer*'s wrist. Hundreds of megajoules burned through what remained of the *Marauder*'s cockpit armor as great green beams of light blazed toward the sky. The 'Mech wavered in place, then collapsed straight down onto its spindly legs, smoke pouring from the remains of its head.

Great, gasping breaths tore up Percy's lungs. He'd lost a few heat sinks, and the old 'Mech's cockpit broiled. He popped the canopy and breathed deeply of the cool night air. No signs of battle reached him, only the sizzle and pop of cooling metal, and wind that smelled of imminent rain.

When he could breathe again, Percy clicked on his comm. "Pritchard! Idania! Anyone..."

It was Sid who answered. "They live. The day is ours. The enemy is fleeing with three damaged 'Mechs," He paused. "Brother Perseus, I cannot contact the Red Raven."

Percy flipped to the frequency he shared with Lucien Clearwater and called for him. Lucien always answered him on this band. Tonight, he did not. "Sid, where was he last?"

"North of here. He was chasing something. He sounded... not himself."

Damn it. Percy called up an overhead map of the Draw and headed north. The area was blessedly devoid of heavy minerals, making magnetic scans his best choice.

He searched for half an hour, until a blip appeared on his sensors. It was Lucien's *White Raven,* standing near the edge of the Draw, where a slope ran upward to the ridge line. It appeared intact; nothing had penetrated its ferro-lamellor skin.

"Lucien?" The 'Mech was shut down. Was he out taking another long piss? Percy flicked on his external speakers. "Lucien!"

He walked up to the *White Raven* and shone a light on it. Cold crept up his spine. The cockpit was sealed. He could see inside, to the nothingness therein. "Lucien?"

There came a crackle of static, and within it were words like little talons clawing at his eardrums. *"I am grateful to you, but come no farther."*

The voice was not coming over the comm. Percy took a step closer to the *White Raven.* The voice came from Lucien's 'Mech, from its external speakers.

"Grateful?"

"I've wanted that imposter dead for some time, but she was elusive. Mobile. Smart. Now I can move on to other things."

"Who is this?"

A mechanical crackle of laughter. *"You've been looking for me a long time, Perseus Schell. All that time you spent looking ahead, but you never once looked behind."*

Percy spun around, dropping his 'Mech to one knee. Behind was only darkness, and the ridge line cutting across to the southeast. Lightning illuminated the clouds with bluish-white spiderwebs. There was something up there, something blacker than the darkness. His sensors showed only fuzz, but he saw...a silhouette? Darker. It stole the light, gobbling it up like a miser snatching a penny. It was a hole in reality into which things fell, never to be released.

Percy's instinct was to shoot it, banish it in a blazing fireball, but he'd spent his last missiles on the false *Marauder.* Almost. A round of flare LRMs sat in his right torso. He sent them skyward, and twenty little pops banished the dark of Novo Franklin. But the deeper darkness, the one that seemed to suck out his mind and his courage, that one remained and took shape. Percy's blood ran cold.

He knew the shape. He'd long ago memorized every bizarre angle, every unexpected curve and bulge of it.

"I will allow that, Brother Perseus, for the service you have rendered me." The voice crackling over Lucien's external speakers lacked emotion and patience. *"Do not pursue me any further. My grace has limits, as your Clan friend learned. Keep his 'Mech as a reminder."*

"Lucien—" Percy's throat seized. There were things Lucien had tried to tell him, but he was too thick-skulled to pick up on them. Things the Red Raven had feared. Now he was gone, and Percy was alone, out of range, out of ammo. Even his faith had abandoned him as he stared down... "Who are you?"

"Never ask a question when you fear the answer. Goodbye, Perseus Schell."

The Dark One turned and vanished over the ridge, leaving behind its defeated opponents. Percy could only watch, and weep.

BUCCANEER-CLASS DROPSHIP *CASSIEL*
NOVO FRANKLIN
THE PERIPHERY
20 JULY 3151

Idania's 'Mech was salvageable, Pritchard's not so much. That was fine. He'd wanted a newer 'Mech, so he could take Lucien's *White Raven* once he was back on his feet.

Salvage vehicles from the neighboring fiefs had descended on the Carlton Draw like eager vultures, exchanging small-arms fire as they hauled away the still-smoking corpses of the pirate 'Mechs. Percy let them have everything except the false Langstrom's *Marauder*. That one he would keep, as a remembrance. There was no point in chasing the shadow Percy had seen atop that ridge. An unknown DropShip left the atmosphere that night, its trajectory coming from the wilds. Someone had departed Novo Franklin without doing any trading, and it wasn't hard to guess who.

Percy ordered the *Cassiel*'s crew to barter passage back to Randis IV. The Grand Knight and the Council would expect a report. They would expect success, and he did have that. They had confirmed Brother Thaddeus' fate, retrieved his 'Mech, and ensured the responsible party would plague Novo Franklin no more.

But Percy was not satisfied. Many new pages had been added to his little black notebook, many more questions with answers yet to uncover. And one that had been answered. Percy was now tasked to go forth and tell the galaxy that the Dark One had returned. But who would believe him?

He met with Pritchard, recovering in the *Cassiel*'s medical bay with Idania hovering over him, to tell them his plans. "I am proud of you both. I have written my report for the Council, and I am recommending you both for full knighthood. You'll still have trials to face, but you have my blessing."

They thanked him. Each was happy, yet humble, and that was good. They were learning.

"You can return to Randis," he said, "but I won't be going back. My mission isn't finished. You know what I saw. It's your choice whether to believe me or not.

"I believe you," Idania said. She had no proof, as Percy's battleROM recorded nothing, but she had faith. And she knew truth when it spoke to her.

Pritchard had a different method. He shifted in his bed. "We couldn't have won without Lucien. He deserves justice. I want to get it for him."

"We're with you Percy. Until the end."

Percy smiled, a great warmth spreading through him.

One of the *Cassiel*'s crew came to get him. Sid and his warriors were outside and wanted a word. Percy went down to greet them. A lucky thirteen remained, of almost fifty.

Sid saluted him. "Our DropShip has left us."

"You want passage back to Raven space? I can certainly do that. You don't even have to ask."

Sid rubbed the back of his neck. He looked like a gigantic child trying to ask for a second dessert. "We came on this mission to die. It was expected of us. We failed, as we failed our mission. We are *solahma*, and *dezgra*. Our Clan has no further use for us and will not welcome us home." His eyes brightened. "You will not give up your hunt for this enemy, *quiaff*?"

"Never."

"Then my *trothkin* and I elect to stay with you, if that is acceptable. Perhaps one day we can gain back some honor in the eyes of our Clan. Until then, we place ourselves under your command."

Percy considered him for a long moment, then clasped his shoulder. "Bargained well and done."

"Hit me."

"Why?"

"It is customary." Sid shifted his eyes to his men. "For their benefit."

Percy had trained in several martial disciplines, including some that broke bricks. Driving his fist into Sid's solar plexus was akin to that, but it hurt more. Sid let out his breath in an explosive grunt and collapsed onto his rump. Percy grinned. Sid was a good actor.

Sid rose and brushed himself off. "So, what unit do we now belong to? Something Randis?"

"No." A bittersweet smile grace Percy's lips. "We are the Red Ravens."

He turned, and shifted into a new phase of life. Nothing had changed, but all was different. The sunlight was tinged, impure, like looking though a haze of smog, but Percy would cleanse it. Purpose and certainty burned within in him. He looked to the sky, to the deep. Somewhere out there, somehow, he would find the source of the taint, and he would purify it.

The future beckoned.

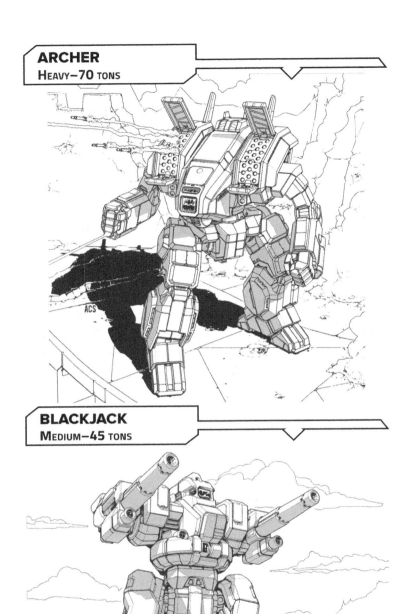

ARCHER
Heavy—70 tons

ACS

BLACKJACK
Medium—45 tons

CHAMELEON
MEDIUM—50 TONS

DERVISH
MEDIUM—55 TONS

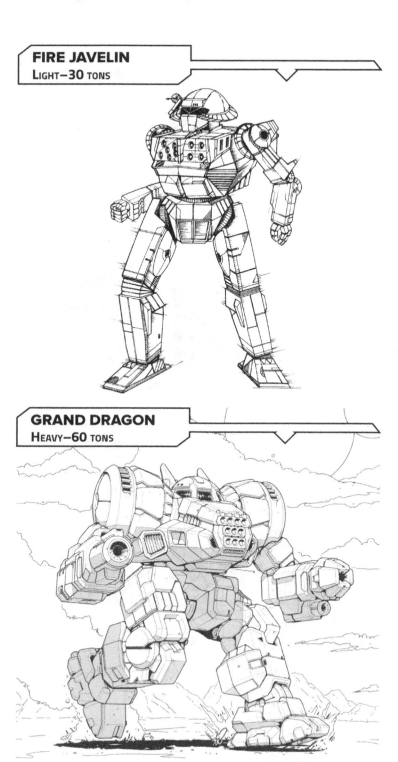

FIRE JAVELIN
LIGHT—30 TONS

GRAND DRAGON
HEAVY—60 TONS

GUILLOTINE
HEAVY—70 TONS

LOCUST
LIGHT—20 TONS

MARAUDER
HEAVY—75 TONS

ROKUROKUBI
LIGHT—35 TONS

SCARABUS
LIGHT—30 TONS

VALKYRIE
LIGHT—30 TONS

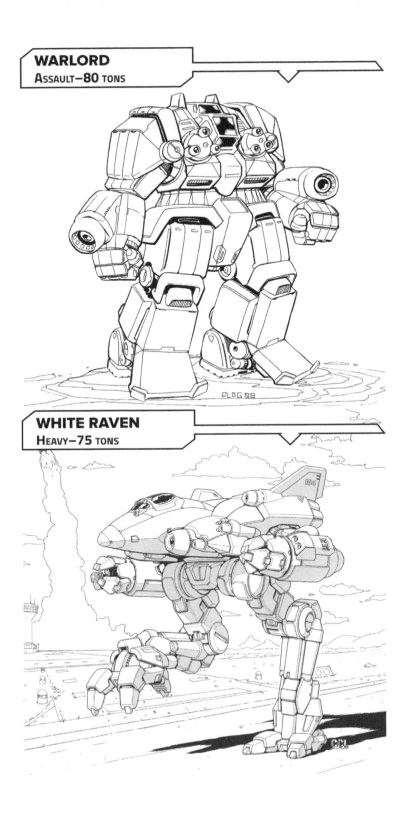

WARLORD
ASSAULT—80 TONS

WHITE RAVEN
HEAVY—75 TONS

BATTLETECH GLOSSARY

AUTOCANNON

A rapid-fire, auto-loading weapon. Light autocannons range from 30 to 90 millimeter (mm), and heavy autocannons may be from 80 to 120mm or more. They fire high-speed streams of high-explosive, armor-piercing shells.

BATTLEMECH

BattleMechs are the most powerful war machines ever built. First developed by Terran scientists and engineers, these huge vehicles are faster, more mobile, better-armored and more heavily armed than any twentieth-century tank. Ten to twelve meters tall and equipped with particle projection cannons, lasers, rapid-fire autocannon and missiles, they pack enough firepower to flatten anything but another BattleMech. A small fusion reactor provides virtually unlimited power, and BattleMechs can be adapted to fight in environments ranging from sun-baked deserts to subzero arctic icefields.

DROPSHIPS

Because interstellar JumpShips must avoid entering the heart of a solar system, they must "dock" in space at a considerable distance from a system's inhabited worlds. DropShips were developed for interplanetary travel. As the name implies, a DropShip is attached to hardpoints on the JumpShip's drive core, later to be dropped from the parent vessel after in-system entry. Though incapable of FTL travel, DropShips are highly maneuverable, well-armed and sufficiently aerodynamic to take off from and land on a planetary surface. The journey from the jump point to the inhabited worlds of a system usually requires a normal-space journey of several days or weeks, depending on the type of star.

FLAMER

Flamethrowers are a small but time-honored anti-infantry weapon in vehicular arsenals. Whether fusion-based or fuel-based, flamers spew fire in a tight beam that "splashes" against a target, igniting almost anything it touches.

GAUSS RIFLE

This weapon uses magnetic coils to accelerate a solid nickel-ferrous slug about the size of a football at an enemy target, inflicting massive damage through sheer kinetic impact at long range and with little heat. However, the accelerator coils and the slug's supersonic speed mean that while the Gauss rifle is smokeless and lacks the flash of an autocannon, it has a much more potent report that can shatter glass.

INDUSTRIALMECH

Also known as WorkMechs or UtilityMechs, they are large, bipedal or quadrupedal machines used for industrial purposes (hence the name). They are similar in shape to BattleMechs, which they predate, and feature many of the same technologies, but are built for non-combat tasks such as construction, farming, and policing.

JUMPSHIPS

Interstellar travel is accomplished via JumpShips, first developed in the twenty-second century. These somewhat ungainly vessels consist of a long, thin drive core and a sail resembling an enormous parasol, which can extend up to a kilometer in width. The ship is named for its ability to "jump" instantaneously across vast distances of space. After making its jump, the ship cannot travel until it has recharged by gathering up more solar energy.

The JumpShip's enormous sail is constructed from a special metal that absorbs vast quantities of electromagnetic energy from the nearest star. When it has soaked up enough energy, the sail transfers it to the drive core, which converts it into a space-twisting field. An instant later, the ship arrives at the next jump point, a distance of up to thirty light-years. This field is known as hyperspace, and its discovery opened to mankind the gateway to the stars.

JumpShips never land on planets. Interplanetary travel is carried out by DropShips, vessels that are attached to the JumpShip until arrival at the jump point.

LASER

An acronym for "Light Amplification through Stimulated Emission of Radiation." When used as a weapon, the laser damages the target by concentrating extreme heat onto a small area. BattleMech lasers are designated as small, medium or large. Lasers are also available as shoulder-fired weapons operating from a portable backpack power unit. Certain range-finders and targeting equipment also employ low-level lasers.

LRM

Abbreviation for "Long-Range Missile," an indirect-fire missile with a high-explosive warhead.

MACHINE GUN

A small autocannon intended for anti-personnel assaults. Typically non-armor-penetrating, machine guns are often best used against infantry, as they can spray a large area with relatively inexpensive fire.

PARTICLE PROJECTION CANNON (PPC)

One of the most powerful and long-range energy weapons on the battlefield, a PPC fires a stream of charged particles that outwardly functions as a bright blue laser, but also throws off enough static discharge to resemble a bolt of manmade lightning. The kinetic and heat impact of a PPC is enough to cause the vaporization of armor and structure alike, and most PPCs have the power to kill a pilot in his machine through an armor-penetrating headshot.

SRM

The abbreviation for "Short-Range Missile," a direct-trajectory missile with high-explosive or armor-piercing explosive warheads. They have a range of less than one kilometer and are only reliably accurate at ranges of less than 300 meters. They are more powerful, however, than LRMs.

SUCCESSOR LORDS

After the fall of the first Star League, the remaining members of the High Council each asserted his or her right to become First Lord. Their star empires became known as the Successor States and the rulers as Successor Lords. The Clan Invasion temporarily interrupted centuries of warfare known as the Succession Wars, which first began in 2786.

BATTLETECH ERAS

The *BattleTech* universe is a living, vibrant entity that grows each year as more sourcebooks and fiction are published. A dynamic universe, its setting and characters evolve over time within a highly detailed continuity framework, bringing everything to life in a way a static game universe cannot match.

To help quickly and easily convey the timeline of the universe—and to allow a player to easily "plug in" a given novel or sourcebook—we've divided *BattleTech* into eight major eras.

STAR LEAGUE
(Present–2780)

Ian Cameron, ruler of the Terran Hegemony, concludes decades of tireless effort with the creation of the Star League, a political and military alliance between all Great Houses and the Hegemony. Star League armed forces immediately launch the Reunification War, forcing the Periphery realms to join. For the next two centuries, humanity experiences a golden age across the thousand light-years of human-occupied space known as the Inner Sphere. It also sees the creation of the most powerful military in human history.

(This era also covers the centuries before the founding of the Star League in 2571, most notably the Age of War.)

SUCCESSION WARS
(2781–3049)

Every last member of First Lord Richard Cameron's family is killed during a coup launched by Stefan Amaris. Following the thirteen-year war to unseat him, the rulers of each of the five Great Houses disband the Star League. General Aleksandr Kerensky departs with eighty percent of the Star League Defense Force beyond known space and the Inner Sphere collapses into centuries of warfare known as the Succession Wars that will eventually result in a massive loss of technology across most worlds.

CLAN INVASION
(3050–3061)

A mysterious invading force strikes the coreward region of the Inner Sphere. The invaders, called the Clans, are descendants of Kerensky's SLDF troops, forged into a society dedicated to becoming the greatest fighting force in history. With vastly superior technology and warriors, the Clans conquer world after world. Eventually this outside threat will forge a new Star League, something hundreds of years of warfare failed to accomplish. In addition, the Clans will act as a catalyst for a technological renaissance.

CIVIL WAR
(3062–3067)

The Clan threat is eventually lessened with the complete destruction of a Clan. With that massive external threat apparently neutralized, internal conflicts explode around the Inner Sphere. House Liao conquers its former Commonality, the St. Ives Compact; a rebellion of military units belonging to House Kurita sparks a war with their powerful border enemy, Clan Ghost Bear; the fabulously powerful Federated Commonwealth of House Steiner and House Davion collapses into five long years of bitter civil war.

JIHAD
(3067–3080)
Following the Federated Commonwealth Civil War, the leaders of the Great Houses meet and disband the new Star League, declaring it a sham. The pseudo-religious Word of Blake—a splinter group of ComStar, the protectors and controllers of interstellar communication—launch the Jihad: an interstellar war that pits every faction against each other and even against themselves, as weapons of mass destruction are used for the first time in centuries while new and frightening technologies are also unleashed.

DARK AGE
(3081–3150)
Under the guidance of Devlin Stone, the Republic of the Sphere is born at the heart of the Inner Sphere following the Jihad. One of the more extensive periods of peace begins to break out as the 32nd century dawns. The factions, to one degree or another, embrace disarmament, and the massive armies of the Succession Wars begin to fade. However, in 3132 eighty percent of interstellar communications collapses, throwing the universe into chaos. Wars erupt almost immediately, and the factions begin rebuilding their armies.

ILCLAN
(3151–present)
The once-invulnerable Republic of the Sphere lies in ruins, torn apart by the Great Houses and the Clans as they wage war against each other on a scale not seen in nearly a century. Mercenaries flourish once more, selling their might to the highest bidder. As Fortress Republic collapses, the Clans race toward Terra to claim their long-denied birthright and create a supreme authority that will fulfill the dream of Aleksandr Kerensky and rule the Inner Sphere by any means necessary: The ilClan.

CLAN HOMEWORLDS
(2786–present)
In 2784, General Aleksandr Kerensky launched Operation Exodus, and led most of the Star League Defense Force out of the Inner Sphere in a search for a new world, far away from the strife of the Great Houses. After more than two years and thousands of light years, they arrived at the Pentagon Worlds. Over the next two-and-a-half centuries, internal dissent and civil war led to the creation of a brutal new society—the Clans. And in 3049, they returned to the Inner Sphere with one goal—the complete conquest of the Great Houses.

LOOKING FOR MORE HARD HITTING BATTLETECH FICTION?

WE'LL GET YOU RIGHT BACK INTO THE BATTLE!

Catalyst Game Labs brings you the very best in *BattleTech* fiction, available at most ebook retailers, including Amazon, Apple Books, Kobo, Barnes & Noble, and more!

NOVELS

1. *Decision at Thunder Rift* by William H. Keith Jr.
2. *Mercenary's Star* by William H. Keith Jr.
3. *The Price of Glory* by William H. Keith, Jr.
4. *Warrior: En Garde* by Michael A. Stackpole
5. *Warrior: Riposte* by Michael A. Stackpole
6. *Warrior: Coupé* by Michael A. Stackpole
7. *Wolves on the Border* by Robert N. Charrette
8. *Heir to the Dragon* by Robert N. Charrette
9. *Lethal Heritage* (The Blood of Kerensky, Volume 1) by Michael A. Stackpole
10. *Blood Legacy* (The Blood of Kerensky, Volume 2) by Michael A. Stackpole
11. *Lost Destiny* (The Blood of Kerensky, Volume 3) by Michael A. Stackpole
12. *Way of the Clans* (Legend of the Jade Phoenix, Volume 1) by Robert Thurston
13. *Bloodname* (Legend of the Jade Phoenix, Volume 2) by Robert Thurston
14. *Falcon Guard* (Legend of the Jade Phoenix, Volume 3) by Robert Thurston
15. *Wolf Pack* by Robert N. Charrette
16. *Main Event* by James D. Long
17. *Natural Selection* by Michael A. Stackpole
18. *Assumption of Risk* by Michael A. Stackpole
19. *Blood of Heroes* by Andrew Keith
20. *Close Quarters* by Victor Milán
21. *Far Country* by Peter L. Rice
22. *D.R.T.* by James D. Long
23. *Tactics of Duty* by William H. Keith
24. *Bred for War* by Michael A. Stackpole
25. *I Am Jade Falcon* by Robert Thurston
26. *Highlander Gambit* by Blaine Lee Pardoe
27. *Hearts of Chaos* by Victor Milán
28. *Operation Excalibur* by William H. Keith
29. *Malicious Intent* by Michael A. Stackpole
30. *Black Dragon* by Victor Milán
31. *Impetus of War* by Blaine Lee Pardoe
32. *Double-Blind* by Loren L. Coleman
33. *Binding Force* by Loren L. Coleman
34. *Exodus Road* (Twilight of the Clans, Volume 1) by Blaine Lee Pardoe
35. *Grave Covenant* ((Twilight of the Clans, Volume 2) by Michael A. Stackpole

76. *Daughter of the Dragon* by Ilsa J. Bick
77. *Heretic's Faith* by Randall N. Bills
78. *Fortress Republic* by Loren L. Coleman
79. *Blood Avatar* by Ilsa J. Bick
80. *Trial by Chaos* by J. Steven York
81. *Principles of Desolation* by Jason M. Hardy and Randall N. Bills
82. *Wolf Hunters* by Kevin Killiany
83. *Surrender Your Dreams* by Blaine Lee Pardoe
84. *Dragon Rising* by Ilsa J. Bick
85. *Masters of War* by Michael A. Stackpole
86. *A Rending of Falcons* by Victor Milán
87. *Pandora's Gambit* by Randall N. Bills
88. *A Bonfire of Worlds* by Steven Mohan, Jr.
89. *Isle of the Blessed* by Steven Mohan, Jr.
90. *Embers of War* by Jason Schmetzer
91. *Betrayal of Ideals* by Blaine Lee Pardoe
92. *Forever Faithful* by Blaine Lee Pardoe
93. *Kell Hounds Ascendant* by Michael A. Stackpole
94. *Redemption Rift* by Jason Schmetzer
95. *Grey Watch Protocol* (*The Highlander Covenant, Book One*)
     by Michael J. Ciaravella
96. *Honor's Gauntlet* by Bryan Young
97. *Icons of War* by Craig A. Reed, Jr.
98. *Children of Kerensky* by Blaine Lee Pardoe
99. *Hour of the Wolf* by Blaine Lee Pardoe
100. *Fall From Glory* (*Founding of the Clans, Book One*) by Randall N. Bills
101. *Paid in Blood* (*The Highlander Covenant, Book Two*) by Michael J. Ciaravella
102. *Blood Will Tell* by Jason Schmetzer
103. *Hunting Season* by Philip A. Lee
104. *A Rock and a Hard Place* by William H. Keith, Jr.
105. *Visions of Rebirth* (Founding of the Clans, Book Two) by Randall N. Bills
106. *No Substitute for Victory* by Blaine Lee Pardoe
107. *Redemption Rites* by Jason Schmetzer
108. *Land of Dreams* (Founding of the Clans, Book Three) by Randall N. Bills

YOUNG ADULT NOVELS

1. *The Nellus Academy Incident* by Jennifer Brozek
2. *Iron Dawn* (*Rogue Academy, Book 1*) by Jennifer Brozek
3. *Ghost Hour* (*Rogue Academy, Book 2*) by Jennifer Brozek
4. *Crimson Night* (*Rogue Academy, Book 3*) by Jennifer Brozek

OMNIBUSES

1. *The Gray Death Legion Trilogy* by William H. Keith, Jr.
2. *The Blood of Kerensky Trilogy* by Michael A. Stackpole

NOVELLAS/SHORT STORIES

1. *Lion's Roar* by Steven Mohan, Jr.
2. *Sniper* by Jason Schmetzer
3. *Eclipse* by Jason Schmetzer
4. *Hector* by Jason Schmetzer
5. *The Frost Advances (Operation Ice Storm, Part 1)* by Jason Schmetzer
6. *The Winds of Spring (Operation Ice Storm, Part 2)* by Jason Schmetzer
7. *Instrument of Destruction (Ghost Bear's Lament, Part 1)*
   by Steven Mohan, Jr.
8. *The Fading Call of Glory (Ghost Bear's Lament, Part 2)* by Steven Mohan, Jr.
9. *Vengeance* by Jason Schmetzer
10. *A Splinter of Hope* by Philip A. Lee
11. *The Anvil* by Blaine Lee Pardoe
12. *A Splinter of Hope/The Anvil* (omnibus)
13. *Not the Way the Smart Money Bets (Kell Hounds Ascendant #1)*
    by Michael A. Stackpole
14. *A Tiny Spot of Rebellion (Kell Hounds Ascendant #2)*
    by Michael A. Stackpole
15. *A Clever Bit of Fiction (Kell Hounds Ascendant #3)* by Michael A. Stackpole
16. *Break-Away (Proliferation Cycle #1)* by Ilsa J. Bick
17. *Prometheus Unbound (Proliferation Cycle #2)* by Herbert A. Beas II
18. *Nothing Ventured (Proliferation Cycle #3)* by Christoffer Trossen
19. *Fall Down Seven Times, Get Up Eight (Proliferation Cycle #4)* by Randall N. Bills
20. *A Dish Served Cold (Proliferation Cycle #5)*
    by Chris Hartford and Jason M. Hardy
21. *The Spider Dances (Proliferation Cycle #6)* by Jason Schmetzer
22. *Shell Games* by Jason Schmetzer
23. *Divided We Fall* by Blaine Lee Pardoe
24. *The Hunt for Jardine (Forgotten Worlds, Part One)* by Herbert A. Beas II
25. *Rock of the Republic* by Blaine Lee Pardoe
26. *Finding Jardine (Forgotten Worlds, Part Two)* by Herbert A. Beas II
27. *The Trickster (Proliferation Cycle #7)* by Blaine Lee Pardoe
28. *The Price of Duty* by Jason Schmetzer
29. *Elements of Treason: Duty* by Craig A. Reed, Jr.
30. *Mercenary's Honor* by Jason Schmetzer

ANTHOLOGIES

1. *The Corps (BattleCorps Anthology, Volume 1)* edited by Loren. L. Coleman
2. *First Strike (BattleCorps Anthology, Volume 2)* edited by Loren L. Coleman
3. *Weapons Free (BattleCorps Anthology, Volume 3)* edited by Jason Schmetzer
4. *Onslaught: Tales from the Clan Invasion* edited by Jason Schmetzer
5. *Edge of the Storm* by Jason Schmetzer
6. *Fire for Effect (BattleCorps Anthology, Volume 4)* edited by Jason Schmetzer

MAGAZINES

The march of technology across BattleTech's eras is relentless...

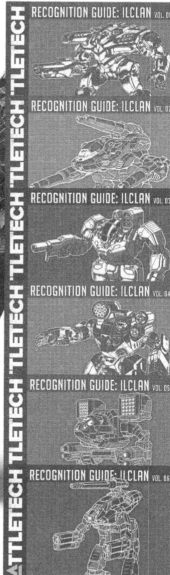

RECOGNITION GUIDE: ILCLAN VOL. 01

RECOGNITION GUIDE: ILCLAN VOL. 02

RECOGNITION GUIDE: ILCLAN VOL. 03

RECOGNITION GUIDE: ILCLAN VOL. 04

RECOGNITION GUIDE: ILCLAN VOL. 05

RECOGNITION GUIDE: ILCLAN VOL. 06

BATTLETECH TLETECH TLETECH TLETECH TLETECH

Some BattleMech designs never die. Each installment of *Recognition Guide: IIClan*, currently a PDF-only series, not only includes a brand new BattleMech or OmniMech, but also details Classic 'Mech designs from both the Inner Sphere and the Clans, now fully rebuilt with Dark Age technology (3085 and beyond).

STORE.CATALYSTGAMELABS.COM

Made in the USA
Monee, IL
13 November 2024

69972653R00085